LIFE 2

By Joe Roach

Cadmuspublishing.com

JOE ROACH

JOE ROACH

LIFE 2

By Joe Roach

DISCLAIMER:
The thoughts, opinions, and expressions herein are those of the author and do not reflect those of Cadmus Publishing LLC. Any similarities to actual events or people are purely coincidental. Names and distinguishing characteristics may have been changed to preserve the identities of any individuals. Published by Cadmus Publishing LLC. P. O. Box 8664. Haledon, NJ 07538
Web: Cadmuspublishing.com
Web: BooksByPrisoners.com
Business email: admin@cadmuspublishing.com
Author email: info@cadmuspublishing.com
Phone: 360.565.6459
ISBN# 978-1-63751-483-2
Book catalog info. Categories. Fiction, Action, Thriller

Cadmuspublishing.com

LIFE 2

TABLE OF CONTENTS

JOE ROACH

Chapter 1 The Outlaw Life

The story that tells about all my love and how the outlaw life really began. The people that say they know me. The only person that really knows me is God.

I've been a cat of many colors. Regardless of what I've done, my heart has never changed. I am a good soft-hearted person that's been through a lot of unnecessary bullshit throughout my life by family. I write my story as fiction to protect me. There are just some stories I can't make up. You can be the judge of that. To me, it's all fiction. I have a good heart, a loving heart. All my life I've stayed around to show my love to my family. Hopefully to see some in return. That never happened. All through my life, as long as I was doing for others, they didn't mind me being around. They had no problem working me like a slave. Giving credit to the one they loved when others were around. As soon as I'd leave from their site. After helping all day, they'd say to one another: He wants something. If not, he wouldn't be around. Maybe a little love would have been a lot when you showed me none my whole life. Instead, you'd rather me not come around at all. That worked out great for the ones that got all the love. They got all the love and all the credit.

I continue to be an outcast, when I'd get angry and mad, because it was plain to see what was going on. I was told, "Joe, if you don't like it, don't come around." Instead of listening to what had been said to me, I continued to come around trying to force my family to love me. They had no love for me. They'd rather me not be around. That way, they didn't have to say no if I asked for anything. Because if I did that would be the answer I got, "No!" People don't know the real facts of life, and never will. As long as I'm not around, that's the way my family likes it and would like to keep it that way. As for being a part of the family tree, I was cut from that the day I came into this world. That's what a child gets when he or she is unwanted to begin with. Being born only eleven months after the promise child, you get to know that was an accident. The birth control didn't have a chance to kick in.

I'm not sure they had birth control back then. I know my life has been nothing but a train wreck. Out of thirty kids raised in

LIFE 2

Roach Town, I was the only one to turn out like this. That should tell everyone. It's something wrong with this picture.

You would think I'd done something bad. All I have had was a heart full of love to share to get nothing in return. A lot of abuse growing up, some of the abuse no child could ever ask for. Being the outcast I was, if I said anything to my parents, it would have only brought problems for them, cuz my whole life I've been made out to be nothing but a liar. When you are labeled that kind of a child, that opens the door for a lot of messed up stuff to go on. And it did. All I could do was go with it and keep my mouth shut. That's what I learned throughout my childhood from the beatings I got. No matter what was happening to me, I done it to myself, or I was nothing but a lair. So it's best to keep my mouth shut. This was my real Roach Town childhood.

I don't think my mom and dad wanted it to be that way. To satisfy others, that's just the way it was. When I got to be a teenager, the less they done for me, made me have to do more for myself. That would bring me a lot of problems. That would be a way to get rid of me. And that's what happened. No matter who was involved in the trouble I got into, I got blamed and was told to take the blame. I was labeled trouble to begin with by the rest of the family. After staying in a boys' home from the time I was thirteen until I was sixteen for helping one of the biggest pieces of shit cousin of mine steal the car rims I've spoke about, I got out. Of course, he never got charged. He was an adult and the king of Roach Town's son. I was just a kid and they made me out to be the biggest piece of shit in Roach Town. What did I do? Steal the rims and roll them from Altavista back to Roach Town at thirteen years old. That's pretty much how it was made out. My uncle said I sold his son the rims. And I was told to go with that. And I did.

My dad knew it was not right. Sometimes you got to do what you got to do to keep trouble down. Dad and mom made sure I was well taken care of in the boys' home by an older black lady that worked there. I would say the most love I ever felt from my mom and dad was when I was locked up. It seems like as long as I was out of sight and out of mind, everyone was happy, no matter the cost. They were happy to pay it to know I was safe and well. That's the love I felt. The young black lady, maybe twenty-eight years old, was everything to me. She was a sweet mother figure. And the best sex I ever had, being the first piece of ass I had at age thirteen. Her name was Karen. She made my life about the happiest I've ever been. Even though I was away from my family, the love I felt from her was many types of love I knew nothing

4

about. Being protected and loved by her gave me a feeling about black folk that would stick with me for a lifetime.

After feeling the love she showed me, I hated to leave when I turned sixteen. I've got to say to my mom and dad; I have to say thanks. They were the ones to make that possible by putting Karen on payroll. I feel like they knew they could never love me the way they loved my other brothers and sisters. The reason that the love wasn't there and the rest of Roach Town family pretty much forbid me being able to have anything. As long as I was happy with Karen in the boy's home, that's the least they could do. Karen was who I really felt love from. She was good to me. The love others felt never having to take the blame for anything in Roach Town. That's the love I felt in the boys' home. Karen covered my ass, no matter what I got myself into. I was Karen's pet and enjoyed being there with her. That's the sad part. At the same time, it was a good thing.

I learned a lot about what Karen said black women like. I wouldn't change that life experience for nothing. She's the one who told me I was the only white boy she'd ever seen with a brown worm the size of a black boys. I was only thirteen at that time. Later in life, I learned she wasn't lying. White women told me the same thing at the age of sixteen. After I was released from the boys' home, I did get a young girl pregnant with my first son. I mainly like older women, black or white – it didn't matter. I was on a mission to find another mother and lover figure like Karen was. It didn't take me long. I met a middle-aged lady. She was from the Snow Creek area. Being only sixteen, I lied and said I was eighteen the first night we met. She said she was going to give me some pussy. The day I fucked her would determine whether she let me fuck her again. It really surprised her when we got to her house, then got undressed. She said herself I definitely didn't have a young boy's worm. And the color was more than rare. She'd never seen one so brown on a white boy or man before. She was a middle-aged lady, and she had no reason to lie. I'm sure she had seen lots of them throughout her years.

All I done was what Karen taught me to do – that's started off by sucking and licking lips, then her nipple, then every hole below her hips. Karen told me I'd have no problem getting off a black woman, and I'd especially drive a white woman crazy. I can say everything Karen taught me and told me was nothing but the truth. Karen never had a reason to lie to me. As far as I know, she never did. While I'm beating this middle-aged lady's back out from behind, she's saying ooh and all that good shit women do to make a guy think he's doing something. I'm sixteen years old and there's no way I can be doing nothing but heating it up for the next one that's bigger. But anyway, if you want to know about the adventures of the brown worm, I encourage you to read the book I'm going to write called The Brown Worm.

Let's skip the sex part with the middle-aged lady. When we was done that night, at the age of sixteen, I was told I didn't need to worry about going home. I could stay with her. That's where I stayed until I got the robbery charge at age seventeen. I didn't really care as long as I went back to the same boys' home. Back then, you had three picks, meaning I hadn't been out maybe a year. The judge ordered for me to go back there. That's where I asked to be sent. There I was back in the saddle again with really the only person I'd ever felt love from. Then the ten years for the check charge's really the ten years was for being caught with the cop's wife. Tina was the girl that I done that time with. I'm back in prison now doing another ten years. We're not going into that right now. I will say this is about the hardest time I've ever spent. Read the rest of my book and you will figure my life out. Buckle up. You in for a long ride of the craziest and wildest lifestyle that's made a legend out of me. Joe Roach – the one and only real outlaw in five surrounding counties.

Chapter 2 1-5 A Brief Follow Up Why I'm in Prison

After writing my first book about bits and pieces of my life, it turns out to be a best seller. A lot of people bought it like I knew they would. There are a lot of people that knows I'm not really a bad guy. Then you have the haters. They never going to say anything good cuz their life is so miserable. They can't stand that I make the best of mine no matter where I am. A lot of them sit around and make up a lot of stories about me. So unreal people don't really believe them. They just listen to hear just what a hater other people really are. They don't even question half of what they hear. They know better. It just goes in one ear and out the other. The only ones that do listen are haters just like the ones talking. A lot of them are mostly family and lawmen. With it being like this makes it hard to defend myself to the people that don't really know me, like a lot of other people that does. Certain ones in the family does this to keep the lawmen from looking at the dirt they're doing.

The stories that's made up about me is the stories the lawmen want to believe to make their job look so dangerous and what danger they deal with. I'm a wanted man for murder that I knew nothing about. If anyone can convince you I have killed someone, that goes to show you don't know me at all. The lawmen don't mind making me look bad, as long as they look like they are doing their job.

So many stories have been made up about me - the law don't care about the truth. They just want to lock me up just to feel like they done something - the whole time lying to the community, like I really killed somebody, while the community is thinking I'm in prison for murder. I'm really in jail or prison for charges as petty as cashing a stolen check that I never cashed to begin with. Using that I've been arrested for murder to shock the community, saying I blew a guy's head off that I didn't even know. I'm serving ten years for a check and violation of probation. The community never hears about the real reason I'm in prison.

JOE ROACH

My whole life has been an adventure. I've not been an angel. It's hard to be anything close to an angel when my whole life has been full of lies. As for an outlaw life, I can say that's a life I've lived to the fullest – on the run mostly from lies being told more than crimes I committed. I was tracked down like an outlaw and brought to justice. 80% of the crimes I was not convicted of. People say I got off because of money. The real reason was that I knew nothing about the crime. Just lies mainly and most of them came from haters like family members that never wanted me to be a better person. If it wasn't for the lies, my record isn't really that bad. 80% of my charges were dismissed before trial because I never should have been charged to begin with. The lawmen's mission was accomplished. They destroyed my record with dismissed charges that's still held against me anytime I do get in trouble. The violent charges on my record were all dismissed. What petty charges I have been found guilty of anyone else, without my record that shows dismissed charges, would get 30 days. The dismissed charges on my record still count against me because I was charged and run my guidelines up to a ten-year sentence.

That was the lawmen's goal; to use and destroy me and it's worked. I was arrested for murder this time only twelve hours after

LIFE 2

being released from prison. A murder I did not know that had happened at the time. They arrested me for murder that was nothing but a lie a lawman made up to frame me with because he has personal issues with me. When he couldn't charge me with murder, he charged me with receiving stolen property – something I had received before I went to prison. I served the two years and was only out twelve hours before he had me picked back up on the murder charge. He then charges me with the stolen property, and I was sentenced to ten years. That's what I'm serving now. This is the kind of problems I'm having out of certain lawmen that's out for revenge for something that happened twenty years ago. I received ten years back then for revenge. The cop's daddy was a lawman back then and now his son is out for revenge. He tried to take me out for good. He had plotted to frame me for the perfect murder. He just didn't do his homework. If he did, he wouldn't have made an ass out of his self. He would have known that he couldn't frame me. I had just gotten out of prison. The way he had it all laid out for me to have done the murder took a shit in his face. It was no way. But he still got me by lying about stolen property. When a person's record is as altered as mine, I never stood a chance in the courts I was in.

JOE ROACH

While I sit here doing this ten years, I wrote a little about this in my first book called Life. Now I'm going to write Life2, The Outlaw Life. A lot I left out about my life of crime in my first book – true crime fiction. The crimes I committed and the crimes I got away with, none of them are murder. But they are a lot more serious than petty crimes and that's cost me twenty-five years of my life. I'm an outlaw, so everything I say is fiction. Just like the crimes I'm doing ten years for, I'll always say I didn't commit them, petty or not. This is an outlaw's life when the law gets your number, like they've had mine for a long time.

Chapter 3 Now – The Outlaw Life

I think the biggest problem with the law I've played like a game, like cat and mouse with them my whole life. Anytime I wasn't in prison, I was always on the wrong side of the law. As for me being an outlaw, I do believe I've always had the outlaw blood running through my veins. I've had some close calls with the law, but seem to get away with every time, except the lies. I had a criminal mind. You can only imagine what I have got away with. Not many eighteen-year-old puny white boys fresh out of a boys' home for armed robbery. I get plugged in with a world Grade A cocaine supplier out of Miami. I was true and real to the game. I read a book fake while I was locked up about getting out of the game. You got to get into the game first. I'm not fronting or lying, talking about money or riding in a Benz. That's someone that likes to dream about the dope game. I was happy with my 5.0 Foxbody Mustang convertible when I got started bringing twenty kilos at a time from Miami back to my buddy in DOC – run his name as Clinton.

This was the real dope game. I don't have to speak on the bitches I had. With weight like that you already know bitches were everywhere I turn. Just ask anyone that knew me. I always kept the baddest bitch with me, no matter where I went. This book is about the outlaw life of Joe Roach. I had a good run back and forward to Miami. The kilos we were getting were coming from a huge shipment the Feds were letting come into Miami; as much as 40,000 lbs. at a time that came in on a deep sea fishing ship. This Grade A cocaine was meant to be job security for the Feds all across the United States. Clinton was plugged in with the guy that owned the ship. This guy was Clinton's family. The kilos cost us next to nothing. What little we took, the Feds never missed. We took enough to flood four counties. After years of fortune and fame, it ended with a twenty year prison sentence for kingpin charges for trafficking. The only good thing about the law back then is I had to do only a quarter of the time. After five years in Mecklenburg prison, I was released on parole. Thirty days after I

LIFE 2

was released on parole, I was sitting at a stop light in Miami with twenty more kilos in a spare tire in the trunk of a BMW convertible on my way back to the DOC run. That was the balls this outlaw had. This time I was taking a big risk with fifteen years hanging over my head. All I needed was a couple of good licks like this and I'd be set. I'd been set after the first trip, but I had to split it four ways with Clinton and his two brothers. That's the deal we had.

I was either a smart guy with a criminal mind or lucky along with being crazy as hell, I was told. What I like about the lifestyle I was living was the rush I felt and the money I made and knowing I was breaking the law. The blood running through my veins every time I passed a state man on the interstate made me feel like an outlaw that was on the run – just like Billy the Kid after robbing a bank. If only the lawmen knew who I was and the weight I had in that spare tire, I'd be put under the jail. That made the blood pump that much faster through my veins. My mom and dad did not raise me to be this way. They never turned their back on me. I knew they had to wonder what happened. They didn't sign up for me to turn out like this. I can't explain how or why I turned out like I did. My mom and dad have been against drugs and everything else I had seemed to be doing back then.

They talked to me after I served my first five years. Daddy gave me every opportunity to be a part of the family business. Do right and live a good life. If anyone knows my family, they know I have a good hard-working family. That just wasn't the life for me. I was a crook and an outlaw. Fast money was my life. After the taste of easy and fast money when I was young, that took me over. I never cared much for hard work. Breaking the law was much more fun. Plus at this time in my life, there were some lawmen that were outlaws too. That didn't help me none, knowing some of the lawmen and having them on board with what I had going on. I was much younger than the lawmen. The money they made - $25,000 a year – was nothing to the money we all were making. Being outlaws along with them, having a badge, I make a big drug bust and they go take the drugs back to be sold again.

When lawmen get a taste of money like I'm talking, laws are meant to be bent, then broken when it comes to making money. You take a lawman barely getting by on a lawman's pay. A few good licks, they driving new vehicles paid for. Like Billy the Kid said, "With a few good men, you had a posse and a posse with a badge, we could make anything happen." I had my hands in so much, when my buddy John Paul showed up with one of the lawmen at my house to pick me up to go steal a tractor trailer load of Grizzly four-wheelers, I knew then we were doing too much. The truck driver done left the keys over the sun visor of the truck, for $2000, and it was $100,000 worth of four-wheelers still in crates packed in the trailer. You know, we had to get that, with a police escort. One of the biggest heists ever. The next day, we were each $15,000 richer and the lawman, John and I kept us each a brand new 4x4 G4rizzly four-wheeler, then ditched the truck two counties away.

The truck driver that turned us on to the deal, we paid $2,000. I heard later that he lost his job. I know he should have expected that. It was what it was. We all slowed down a lot after this when people started talking. The next thing you know, you got problems.

I ended up taking off to Texas. I didn't take a vehicle. I had my older sister Jenny to take me to the Greyhound station in Vinton, where I took the Greyhound out to Texas. That was a four-day ride. I ended up meeting a girl in Nashville that was riding the bus to Little Rock. She asked me if she could set beside me. I told her "Shore. I'd like that. Give me someone to talk to." Turns out, I didn't get to do much talking. She was a talker. When we got to Little Rock, I ended up getting off with her, where we got a room. You know how, being an outlaw goes. A few days of drinking in every club near the room and we done hooked up with some old school drunk from a motorcycle gang we ran into. We got high as giraffe pussy and fuck like we been knowing each other forever. These were the good outlaw days.

She asked why I was going to Texas. I told her I didn't really have a reason. I was really sightseeing the country and getting a break from Virginia. She asked me if I knew anything about human trafficking. I was honest with her. I did not. She said it was big money, smuggling Mexicans from Mexico on the United States side back to Tennessee. That's the reason she was taking the bus from Nashville. She explained how it works. Hell, that seemed easy enough. She said she had a job lined up if I wanted in on it. From Corpus Christi, Texas back to Virginia. Then I asked what part of Virginia. She said Franklin County. That was one of my counties. I knew a lot of people from there, like Clinton and his brothers. She said the reason she hadn't taken the job was she didn't know much about Virginia at all. Back in those days, Mexicans were worth a lot of money to Tobacco farmers and Dairy farmers. We could get $1,000 a head to smuggle these Mexicans to Virginia in the back of a U-Haul.

LIFE 2

This lady was middle age, so she knew a lot more about what she was talking about, I'm Just killing time let things cool down, Hell I'm game if she wanted to do it. She said if we got caught, we was going to prison for a while, I'm on parole if I got caught out the state I was going back to prison any way. I was an outlaw, I lived on borrowed time anyhow, she called the guy he lived in Texas, He told her he had Ten Mexicans, The Coyotes could have there in Corpus Cristie by time we got there. The have the U-Haul ready. I'm not sharing what he charged the Mexicans, when we got them to the farmer the farmer paid us $ 1,000 each in cash,

The next day we took the Greyhound from little rock to Corpus Cristie Texas, just outside of Fort Hood army base. Took us almost a day and a half before we arrived, when we pulled on up on the bus, we were within walking distance to where we needed to be. There was a U-Haul sitting out front of a two-story apartment building apartment #22 Pam is the girl I'm with, she knocks on the door, then a Mexican girl comes to the door speaking Spanish, Pam speaks Spanish to her then we go inside. The Mexican's are there waiting. The apartment is nasty like I've never seen so nasty, Mexican's live that way, found out there were ten Mexican men there, age from twenty-five to thirty-five They looked kinda afraid Pam talked to them and let them know we were there to take them to Va. They lightened up after Pam spoke with them. All Mexicans like White Women. Pam was a pretty woman and carried herself pretty slutty with long red hair and Double D titties, and a pistol in her boot at all times, she was outlaw herself.

The U-Haul set up was pretty sweet, It was stack with boxes about half way from the back forward they climb through into the opening part where there were a small sofa and couple chairs, you would never know it was there it look like it was loaded with boxes, close to a three days ride none stop Just to get fuel that's it, the Mexican never seen the outside again until we pull into the farm in Snow Creek. on the back of the tobacco farm was a couple older mobile homes that's where they got out unloaded the boxes and the sofa and chairs, Pam collected the $10,000 in cash from the farmer. Then we left I knew the farmer personally; we left the farm tum the U-Haul back into a U-Haul rental place not far from the Greyhound station in Vinton. First, we got a cab to Days Inn, where we caught up on our sleep for a couple days, then went to a couple clubs after catching up on our sleep, had some drinks ate good at this one place called Corn Beef. After a few days Pam took the Greyhound back to Little Rock, I stayed in Va got my sister to pick me up.

LIFE 2

What a story I had to tell. This was some real outlaw days. After getting back to my place in Roachtown, I went to visit my mom and dad at their lake house. They never ask me much about what I been doing or what I had going on because the rather not know. They said that way they never had to worry about answering any questions, If the law showed up with questions about me or my whereabouts. As he sat on the front porch of his mom and dads lake house, Joes the biggest outlaw in Belford co. There was a lot more traffic on his dads road than he ever remember it being, with the lake being built and the northerner's crowding in Joe was an outlaw these northerner's would never forget. They started this war, the south rises again.

Most people can spot an outlaw from a mile away. Joe Roach was never one of the outlaw's that could be spotted from a distance, Joe was the type outlaw that would remind you of the story, sleeping with the enemy. In community's and towns like he was raise in back then lawmen were outlaws too, well let's say a few of them were, and when you got a few good lawmen, Like the sheriff and his handpicked select outlaw lawmen, Billy the Kid would say you got your self your own posse or pack! After Smith Mt. Lake was built that's when things started happing for the better and some for the worse. The people from up north were buying up the lake property as soon as it hit the market for sale with intentions of pushing the middle class out, of course in their eyes we were nothing but trash, you know the south has never took just a minute to look at the real picture, All I'm saying you got to know what you looking for you also got to know a little about the history between the north and the south.

You know the old saying the south will rise again. Why would we want to? The north can have that victory. If it wasn't for them coming for what turn's out to been the biggest thorn in the souths side, There's no way the south could or would have turned out as beautiful as it did. The south looks at the picture like it should be looked at, sometimes you got to lose to win. When the north march away with the nigro's they free from being slaves, the better part of the nigro's stayed. They are not as stupid as the north was, Thay know the south is where they belong, the one's we wanted to stay. A deal had already been made with the ones that wanted to stay, to become sharecroppers after forcing the north to come for what they wanted, the victory was given to them, so they could take the burden out of the souths side so we could rebuild the south into the south it is today. Shortly after the victory the north was too proud to admit the south pull the wool over there eye's. They knew the real victory was in the south. They had created the biggest burden the north has ever created for their self.

LIFE 2

Thats the real reason they were buying up. the lake property, paying ten times the price the property was worth. To get away from the problems they had created for themselves up north. While I sat on my dad's porch at his lake house, watching the people from up north pass by I threw up my hand, they just kept their noses held high like I was some shit. My dad tells me you are wasting your time, they're never going to throw their hand up, they think that they better than we are. Then I explain to my dad that's not true. The reason they don't throw there had up is because they are mad at the south, we fucked them and tricked them into coming down here, using them to take the thorn out of our side and put it in their own side, that's why they are back trying to buy up the most beautiful lake property in the South, Smith Mt Lake. To get away from the disaster they created for the north their own self. For them to think we are their enemy we are not, a man's worse enemy is his best friend. How many of these black folk up north, give a damn about the white folk up north? None All the respect is in the south, where the good white and black folk work things out.

Now let's get back to the real truth and the outlaws that made share Smith Mt Lake got paid, for what the people from the north thought they were not planning to pay the south a dime of their money to help the south. Watching from my dad's porch at Smith Mt. Lake at contractor's run up and down the road, building these homes for the people from up north. I notice none of these contractors were from Va, they all were from up north. It was plain to see the northerners were not going to spend a dime of their money with any southern contractors. At this time, I didn't have much of an education, but it didn't take a rocket scientist to figure out the northerners were trying to put the south out of business. Now remember this beautiful lake was built up by the north but by the south a manmade lake, to attract people from all around "North" "South" "East" and "West". To help build our community into a great and wonderful place to live and come to vacation, there was something wrong with the picture.

The north is having their own contractors to come here and build for them, paying them five times what the south would have charged to build the same home. Now remember this lake stretches through five counties, built by the south with the intention of this lake helping the south contractor's loggers south to build and everyone in the future for the south and their businesses and families. The north was not having it. The north felt the way they were going to get back at us, would be by making sure we did not profit from a dime of their money. The same as starving us out pushing us into poverty. This lake was so big if someone let this go on, they would have done just what they had in mind they were going to do.

LIFE 2

I hadn't been out of prison long maybe a year from a twenty-year sentence for the kingpin act had been sentenced to where took a plea operating a kingpin drug and theft ring. I had not much of a choice but to plea to twenty years, with the agreement I would make parole after serving five years, Thats how I found myself setting on my dad's porch so soon after I was charge with the kingpin act. The lake was really coming along by the northerners around the time I was released on parole. The lawmen that were outlaws, from the beginning respected the way I kept my mouth shut. Why would I involve them, Thay were loyal to me the whole time we were making big money. I kept it real with them by taking the fall being the fall guy. Truth about the matter was I'm the one that got the whole operation tricked up, by thinking with my dick instead of my brain.

I was the one to allow a slut to know too much about what I had going on plus letting a buddy of mine in on the whole operation, I learn a valued lesson. No matter how close you think a buddy is, that buddy will turn out to be your worst enemy. Me and my buddy were so close. We share the same slut at the same time in the same bed. At times we had our dicks in the same time one on the bottom the other behind this slut double penetration.

When I started fucking another girl, the slut gets pissed off, my buddy done fell in love with the slut, him and her together took me out. I was doing things so big back then. They put their self in protective custody afraid I'd have them killed. I could have if I wanted, I had some good Law men that had my back. I never figured it would get as far as it got. To get a charge for being a being a kingpin it got that far out of hand. By then I was in jail being held without bond, for the protection of the commonwealth witness. We all know how that works.

After my buddy took the stand and threw me under every wheel under the bus to be ran over, telling everything he knew and making up what he didn't know, my Lawyer and I decided the twenty-year plea with the understanding I would parole out in five years, was in my best interest to take the plea, because my charges guidelines were twenty to life, that meant the minimum of twenty years and anywhere in between that and the rest of my life I could be sent to prison for.

After sitting on my dad's porch with him watching these northerner's run up and down the road nose in the air still mad at us instead of at their self like they should have been. I'd never known the north to take blame for any wrong. Their education they were so god damn smart even in their mind if they were wrong it was the souths fault they were right. The world really owed them is the way they felt. At this time I wasn't hurting for money. I had about $80,000 in my bank account in a bank in Bedford. That sounds like a lot of money back in 1992 it really wasn't. Maybe to some people, but not to me, I was use to the life I lived before I went to prison that was pocket change.

The lawmen that were outlaws back then they were smart. Making only $ 25,000 a year they knew that wouldn't hardly feed a family. The money they made with me over the few years, from all the kilo's I was hauling in from Miami. They invested their part being smart outlaw men buying land farm cattle farm equipment sawmills every good investment they could make they made. Cause we were doing big, big things back in the eighties. All I cared about was fast cars and fast women. I didn't care about all the material things. I was the kingpin dope man at the time, feeling untouchable and I was at the time. I did do foolish things with my money while everyone else was playing it smart. I get done visiting with my dad so I leave to head back to my place in Roach Town. I notice a sheriff and lawmen at my uncle's house across the Road from my place.

They were my longtime outlaw lawmen. The sheriff said "how are you doing stranger?" I help them load cases of moon shine into the trunk of two police car a Ford LTD back then twenty cases fit in the trunk of a Ford LTD no problem. I ask what about these northerners taking over the lake, not allowing any one from around here to get their money. The sheriff said he had been noticing that. Having a criminal mind like I had all my life, I can change all that. The lawmen were doing good for themselves, now only transporting moon shine now and again, they had already got their selves set from before. They all was going to sit this one out, I think mainly because the heat that was brought the first go around. They survived that only because I took the hit. They knew every lawman other than them was going to have an eye on me to catch me fucking up. The lawmen said do what I wanted to do but if they see me they had to do their job. The biggest word in the world gave me the green light, "If." After the Law men left my uncle said you better be careful you know all the other Law men are out to get you.

I had met this pretty little christian girl name Malinda. She was a beautiful girl. What she seen in me other than being a outlaw I'll never know. We had started dating before I went to prison. Malinda not been involved with the kingpin operation I had going on back then. She knew what I was doing that turn her on for me to be a Bad boy, but to get involved, she didn't want to even hear about it. Even when she made the trips with me to Miami to pick up Ten kilos of Grade A cocaine. She knew but she didn't know if you know what I mean. Malinda was a beautiful girl with a body like most Center folds paid lots of money for, only hers was natural. The first girl I had that wasn't a slut. How that came about I don't know. I would say me getting locked up on the kingpin charge worked out for the best for her if not I would probably turn her into a slut too because that's just how I was. Just like my grandpa said, Roach boys are cursed all they want is a slut, Trust me I believe that I'm not calling nobody else's women a slut. I know a lot about my family, who fuck who and who fuck what. Of course I call all girls sluts cause that's what I love. For the others all I'm saying is if you pick out the sluts there's nothing left, you figure it out. But like I said that's how I feel, my opinion is like an asshole everyone has one. Now I'm out and this little holy girl is back in my life, I heard she fuck at least a half dozen guys while I was in prison is what a guy told me. I told that guy hell that's nothing, that's much better than a good girl hell, six guys five years most time it be five times that many. He said no Joe a half dozen one night beat her back out at a party, I told this guy I don't know what you trying to do. But the more you say about her makes my dick harder and harder! I'll marry this girl. She could be my own personal slut and I'd do just as grandpa said love her forever.

Let's get back to taking care of those contractors. This is our town. We gave the North what they came for the first time, they been crying like bitches ever since. The north are the type no matter how good you are to them, they are never satisfied. Now they think they going to starve us out of our own town. I got something for these mother fuckers. They going to learn how to say thank you with a little respect. The south knows how to stand up. They not letting the north pull the wool over their eyes, I'm a uneducated criminal mind mother fucker. I'm still smart enough to see through this bullshit. I round up a few good outlaws, some I done time with a couple that was kin to me I trusted. Trust me it was only a couple. The rest are snitches. But I learned long ago knowing this is a blessing, family is two headed snakes. The only tail they got is coming out their mouth when they are telling on me.

My uncle knows he said best not let family know a god damn thing. After forming my posse It's time to put a end to the north thinking they got all the sense. If the south can't eat nobody going to eat in the town I was raised in. especially the northerner contractors. I'm depending on this big word "if" to be my green light. And the first night when I had a northerner contractor robbed for all the equipment and utility trailers he had on a job, I was pulling a utility trailer behind my vehicle following the guy on a backhoe when a law man pass. I could see it was one of the good lawmen. He kept on going like he seen nothing. The next day they filed a police report for the northerner for insurance purposes so he could get paid or whoever the rental company could get paid. You would think contractors didn't care insurance was paying. That's true, that's why when you start costing insurance companies a lot of money like contractors getting robbed different ones every night. There were five different counties to choose from, that had northerner contractors

Different county five nights a week until the insurance company finally told the contractors, to leave and if they chose to stay the insurance company was not paying for another thing that got stolen. I didn't stop going back until they all were gone back to where they belong. The northerners did not like it at all. It was what was if you going to live here in our town you going to pay us. I had no problem burning them out if they weren't going to pay. Once a legend for what I done, now a wiped up convicted felon done got old and grey sitting in prison, Telling the stories uncut like it used to be. Back when a good lawman was an outlaw.

Later in the nineties there were a new sheriff come to town, he bought a few fucked up lawmen Just like him along with him how he got in office I don't know.

Still to this day I think he was a god damn northerner. He was a mother fucker. He hated me from the beginning and the feeling for him was mutual. It would not been so bad if he done his job legal like a law man, He was a snake in the grass he was one them snakes with a head on both ends, He had some handpicked law man he brought with him just like him. The only time the public seen this sheriff is when he would be on Tv, lying like a mother fucker about crimes that never happen, He lied to alarm the public, so they send more money. To support the sheriff's office. He was a beggar and a liar never too proud to beg. And too proud to tell the truth. That's type sheriff he was. This sheriff was so sorry, He would steal from himself, when he didn't have to, he was the Sheriff. He would steal anyway. How can you be a sheriff and have a stealing problem. I don't know. I know he stole everything he could get his hands on. All the drugs came up missing from the evidence room, he going to say he destroyed it. Yeah, with them sluts he was paying dope for pussy. That's how it got destroyed. Joe gets into serious trouble and flees to Welch West Va. The untold life the Legend lived over the uncountable years he was hiding out in the deep back woods of West Va, he found his self as an outlaw on the run from Va. For what it seems like one mistake after another. When Joe started digging a hole he never seems to stop until he hit rock bottom.

He came from a good family for the most part except the certain ones in his family that wanted to be lawmen. Joe called them dry snitches. That damage has been done. Joe had found his self in the wrong place one, Indian point Franklin co. Va. Visiting

LIFE 2

What his girlfriend claims to be her friend, straight trash in Joe's eyes.

Joe has been known to mess with some trashy people. He should have known when he seen this girlfriend of his friends that night, she was not the girl for him to have trash like these as friends. Here's the true full effect of how the lights went out at Indian point that night. As soon as Joe follows his girl through the door at her friends place after she had knocked and her lifelong trash said come on in. After Entering the mobile home, she took a seat by her cripple friend that had been cripple for many years and nothing but a drug addict his whole life. Joe stood by the door, He felt bad vibes about the drunken dope heads that were there with this girlfriend's dope head cripple friend. Sorry if this is pissing any one off. The truth is the truth, Joe is calling just like it was, all of these people were trash.

This one guy knew Joe well. He wanted to try Joe. Not only was this guy Grade A number one trash! He thought he was a Bad ass. To hear him tell it he was the baddest S.0.B around. There was only one problem with that piece of trash feeling like he was the Baddest Badass. Joe Roach felt the same damn way about his self, and that guy knew it if he had never been drunk he would never have disrespected Joe Roach by being a dumb mother fucker. This guy gets him a hand full of Joe's girl's titty, then punch Joe in the mouth. Joe and his girl tried to leave. Even though he had disrespect Joe, Joe knew if he didn't get out of there something bad was going to happen. After the guy disrespected Joe, Joe and his girl was leaving, this guy saw Joe didn't want no problem. So now guy going to show off in front of his girlfriend and fuck Joe up.

But what this dumb bad ass mother fucker did not know, He should have left well enough alone, let Joe and his girl leave like they were trying to do. When this guy came around the truck cursing drunk with his girlfriend trying to hold him back like he was a full-blown killer. It's dark and cold out Joe said he will never forget this night. It's a pile of firewood beside Joe's Truck. Joe reaches down get the perfect round hickory stick, the mean mother fucker yea that bad ass. That was dragging his girlfriend around like he was a killer. Ask Donna brown what this full-blown killer said when Joe Roach cut loose beating this trash in the head with the stick of firewood. His tone changed after the first hit to the head. In Joe's mind it was too late for all that please I'm sorry bullshit. Joe beat this mother fucker until he done drop to his knee's a bloody mess, look like something you see in a horror movie. The finale hit was when Joe swung the stick like a ball bat while the trash was beat to his knees. Joe landed the lights out to the side of the guy's head the guy crashing to the ground fall over like a tree.

The guy's girlfriend in screaming, you killed him you kill my boyfriend. Then she turned to run Joe swung the Hickory stick she raised her arm to block it, her arm snapped. Joe could feel it threw the stick, Joe had lost it by now, he beat that whore in the head also until she was unresponsive. Then he got in his truck him and his girl left covered in Blood from the beating he just gave them. He looked like a Serial Killer. Donna didn't know what to think she never seen no one fuck people up that bad in her life. Joe Roach is the only real killer in this town don't forget that. Ask Donna didn't he cry like a slut when I went to his head, he was more of a bitch than his girlfriend. Either I knocked her out with the first hit to the head, or she just laid there why I tried to beat that bitch to death over and over and over licks to the head. I'm not lying ask Donna Brown places I want every one that knows me to know the truth. Joe Roach you do not fuck with, He make the Bad of the Baddest cry like the bitch they are. I hope this pisses you off so you will come back I will do the job right this time. The next time you will not be breathing when I leave you for dead.

If you ever think you going to put your hands on me, you one dead mother fucker. Now let's get back to the night the lights went out of Indian point. So, you will know exactly who you are talking about With No mistakes. If you are not sure look in the mirror at the scars and places where that stick cracked your skull you crying bitch of a man. How you like me now piece of shit?" Knowing he had to get out of town, Donna gets out at his brother's. Joe continues on the run, both pieces of trash live, Joe's Wanted for two count's attempted murder,

Remember this is how fast a sweet night can turn sour!! When you are messing with trash like Donna's So-Called friends this is how it turns out. Especially When Donna's man Joe Roach is the only real killer in town. Don't forget that didn't do you so good to by that night mother fucker, please, please fuck please, you never said please when you thought you was the Badass, member words that out of your mouth you bitch ass mother fucker. Please I'm sorry over and over until the hit to the side of your head shut you the fuck up. You got to be the dumbest mother fucker I know. I got to get away from this life and this state, being wanted and hunted by every very law man in the state.

Joe Roach cuts his hair dyes his brown hair and beard blonde, heads for the wild and wonderful back woods Welch West Va, covered with tattoos from head to toe, Joe look like a criminal offender, Joe had already served five years in prison for a stabbing that left a man dead probably Ten years earlier. Between that and a kingpin drug charge Joe's record wasn't looking good. Not only did he look like a criminal offender his past was proof he was. You would have to know Joe to know he was a good-hearted person. By the sound of the story, he was forced to act like that. It may have gotten a little carried away with the way he beat both of them. The guy asks for it and his girl wouldn't stop screaming. Either way Joe had to shut her up, Before She attracted too much attention to what Just happened by the neighbors. That's the only way Joe would get away from there. He done what he had to do. To a killer once he took one life he Just as well take another, to shut her up that's what he intended to do.

Now in the back woods of West Va, Joe is looking for Work. He's staying at a small Hotel right in the town of Welch. His vehicle is in his sister Jody's name. The Sister that's always tried to keep him out of trouble. This is a long story, now I'm In West Va working. for a guy I knew once before when I was on the run. This time Donna didn't go on the run with me. We had my son Jj and Tosha; my Daughter I wish we would have never went to visit Donna's trashy friend. I tried to tell Donna they were nothing but trash. She said that's what I said about all her friends. We ended up there like I said trash, Donna still thinks I took it a little overboard that night. I feel like they got just what they ask for. I'm staying in a little hotel right in Welch, I was on the logging Job on a Sunday pushing skid rood to get a head start on Monday, Way back in the mountains behind welch. Headed toward Little Davey. Around that evening, I trim the dozer back off the mountain from where I had been punching a road to the landing, I could see a black guy standing at the landing accompanied by a Law man, I was thinking about parking the dozer in the skid road and take off running on foot. Then I thought it must be something other than being there for me. If the law man was there for me for what charges Va had on me, it be every law man in Welch there.

So, I decided to keep my cool find out what was going on. When I got down there, the law man said we had a problem, a rock had rolled off the mountain and knocked a hole in the black guy's sister's house and another had crash into the porch. They think the rocks came from the logging job where I had been pushing back in the mountain. The black guy and I took my vehicle, that was in my sister's name, I'm glad It was so if the law ran the Va tag it come back to her. The black guy and I agree to figure it out thanked the law man, so he left. I was going by Dwayne Smith at this time. The black guy and I rode to his sister's place in Welch where the rocks had rolled from back in the mountain and crash into her house. She stood there with her mom who lived there with her. My boss Tony I used her phone to call. He met me there. Tony talked to Tomica about fixing her house. He had insurance if she wanted someone to fix it, he would turn it in or he have me to fix it and

LIFE 2

pay without turning it in. She said that was fine, only one problem I was not a carpenter. Her brother said he would help me. Tony agrees to pay him. Really, I was going to help him. Tomica like me for some reason. I noticed she had her eye on me for some reason, maybe it was because I was dark tan covered with tattoos. Anyone that knows me knows in the summertime I'm real dark skin and covered from shoulder down with tattoos a complete sleeve shirt. I got all my tattoos my first five years I served at Keen Mt prison kingpin charges.

James was Tomica's brother's name, he lived down the hill from Tomica. Tomica's house was an old coal miner's house built back in the day. Tony told me to start working on the house the next day, James and I stood out by my truck and drank a Bud light I had in the cooler. Tomica looked out a couple times. James said he thought his sister like me. He asked me was I with anyone. He knew from my tags I was from Va. I told him Tony was a good friend I was here working for him, staying at the motel. Tomica looked out the door again, James. yells Tomica come here you know you want to. She said OK I'll be out in a minute give me a minute. James said you she probably putting on some smell good, she's sweet on you Joe. Then he said that is your name right Joe that's what your boss called you, "I said yea" Then he said is it Dwayne that's what you told the lawman. It's Joe I said, he said ok whatever you say. He knew it was something going on with me, I told him what I had going on. I can talk to black folk I've never had black folk to turn me in.

Tomica came out she had a beer with us or two he told Tomica I was renting a room at the hotel by the time I left Tomica told me instead paying for a room I could stay there. It was only her and her mom that lived there. She hadn't been long move there from Alabama to take care her mom. I told her I'd pay her for a room I hated staying by myself at the room, she told me she would ride with me if I wanted to get my things I could start that night staying there. That's the kind of people I always seem to meet, No matter where I was, I've always been a very likeable person, on the way to the room I stop by the store to get us another 12 pack Bud light, she said when I got to the store she needed a couple things was it ok if she got out to come in? I guess she felt being black I'd feel some kind of way. If she thought that she had me confused. I didn't mind at all come on we can walk in together. She said Joe you a funny guy. Not every day in Welch you will see a white guy with a with a black girl. Then she said come to think of it I've never seen that before at all here, you sure you ok with it? Come on girl I hold your hand if you scared, I said, she smiles and then says you are crazy, I open the door. to the store for her she walks in.

Then I walked in behind her of course I had to check that black girl booty out. I was a sucker for black booty, We Just haven't got there far yet I figure after a few more Bud Light's, I'll be done broke the ice to let her in on some my black girl secrets. That always seals the deal, then later just maybe I can be that white boy slave that turns her out by doing to her what the black lady staff taught me black girls like, when I kiss I suck at the same time. All this is crossing my mind as I watch her ass eat up those shorts she's wearing as we make our way back to the truck with the 12 pk plus a few things she needed. I paid for and two pack Newport's one for her and one for me I also paid for, I am a real gentleman when I feel like, if white cracker mother fucker's wouldn't push my buttons I probably be a better person mere often. There sure are some hater white mother fucker's where I come from. By now I'm sure you all know why they are. If you don't know you will shortly, as soon as I get this black girl turn on with the things I'm going to whisper in her ear, as soon as the time is right, the Brown worm is about to strike in Welch West Va. Believe that. All white girls said closest thing to a nigger dick they ever had except for a nigger dick.

For now, I got little more acting right with Tomica We stop by my room first we drink a beer, then I got me a shower, put my boxers on with my dick about half fat I got worked up in the bathroom, before I walk out to get me a pair of jeans while she set on the bed drinking a beer. She said Joe you make me want to be fuck by a white boy so bad come closer let me put my black lips around your dick sure I did Donna I'm sorry you had to find this out twenty years later. Yes, I enjoyed fucking Tomica while I was staying in welch, I know I am a piece of shit, it's hard for me to turn down black pussy. You know I'm telling the truth now twenty year later cause I had your cousin David to help me fix the porch at Tomica's. I could tell everyone how wet that black pussy was in my mouth lips and dick. I figure I'll save them memories for a night when I get out of prison to talk with another Freak. Trust when I say white folk are freaks to especially with me, sky's the limit.

It's hard to say what might come out my mouth. They like it no matter what it is. The only mother fuckers don't like me is little dick law man and all white men. They say I give the white man a bad name. If there were more like me the world would be a better place. Thats not going to happen. There's never going to be another Joe Roach. That's a Fact. The outlaw ways have cost me, Hell someone got to live a life worth writing about, who better to

write about an outlaw life than a real outlaw. That be me Joe
Roach.

Let me tell you about the time I got up one Sunday morning
and showed up at the white folk church my cousin Becky and her
husband Jim invited me to come join them, for Sunday service.
They had invited me some time back. I showed up around 10:45
When I walked in the preacher was preaching, I look around for
Becky & Jim at first I didn't see them, white folks looking at me
like I was lost, I look around for a seat. Everywhere I look they
look at me like I was Forrest Gump on his first day school bus ride.
This seat is taken. I spotted a couple more kin they turn their head
hoping I didn't see them. I did but acted as if I didn't. Then Becky
sees me she and Jim said over here Joe. I took a seat with them.
When I first got there, I think the white folk thought I was an
active shooter. I don't think I was as welcome there as the black
folk church I'd been to with Tomara. As for a hand job that was
dead. I was never welcome, never was I ask to come back, it was
like I wasn't there after they figured out, I wasn't an active gunman
overall it was a good Sunday service.

I was invited to another white folk Church later by another
cousin of mine, her and her husband spotted me when I walked in,
she motions me over to set with her and her family. I see this Law
man there I know. He had stood in front the magistrate one time

and lied through his teeth to make sure I didn't get a bond on a bullshit charge he was involved in having me arrested for. I'm not saying no names, he knows who he is and also, he knows he's a lying piece of shit. I forget when you got a badge and a Christian you can lie. Just ask to be forgiven. No matter how bad a Christian with a badge lies, he can even forget about it. He I guess is still forgiven. He's one of them Law men that has them little boy issues. Every time he goes piss he plays with a little boy dick. We all know now why he's a "Hater." Other than seeing that piece shit in church that was a good and welcome Sunday service. I promise you he most likely had background on me run before Sunday service was over, with hopes I had a warrant so he could arrest me.

Let me tell you what happen later this same day after church, it was later that day around four o'clock I was setting Just below the ATM to the side in my BMW my sister gave me, I was lean over rolling the bubble getting high as giraffe pussy, Rolling the Bubble mean's smoking meth. Before I was about to pull down to the store get some gas and beer. This pretty little young girl pulls beside me, I put the Bubble away roll down my window, she said "are you Joe?" "Yea" I said. She said, "I saw you at church today." "Yea good church service," I said. She said, "What are you doing?" "Getting high I said", she smiled shook her head then said "Everyone says you are crazy. I believe it," she said. She asks what I was doing later, I know this girl, I say to her "you don't want to go there. I'm definitely not your type plus I do not need the trouble." She said, "I'm nineteen, you?" I said and "I'm thirty-seven." She said, "so what does that have to do with us being friends?" She said, "follow me", I said "I got to get gas and beer first", she said "ok then follow me." I pull up to the pump's go pay for the gas and beer get me a pack of smokes, she walks past me never speaks as if she was too good to speak to me in public.

I pump my gas get in put my beer in the cooler start my BMW when I pull off from the pumps, she pulls past me with a smile and points not noticeable to anyone else. She motions for me to follow. I'm thinking what is this girl up to? Fine as a mother fucker phatter than duck butter, nineteen years old I hope this is not a set up. I got a whole ounce of meth in the console; All I need is to get set up by a young church girl. I know her family they are good people. I don't know about all this; I follow her to Moneta then 122 to West Lake we go through the light at West Lake she turns in at Duck in a gas station. She pulls to the far side where there's a park and ride parking. She tells me she was going to walk over to the Lake Inn motel get a room, when I saw her go to the room for me to pull around. I made her promise that this wasn't a set-up, cause that would be so fucked up with me having dope. She reaches in the car kiss me on my lips then she said I want you to fuck the Hell out of me with that mule dick everyone be talks about. Now when I get in the room, I'll leave the door open pull around ok, she said. "Ok I said." I love her already.

When I got to the room, I got my dope and my bubble I walk in at first, I got high as a mother fucker, she wasn't playing. It wasn't no wanting to make love, she was too young for that, me being as high as giraffe pussy, I fuck the brakes of this little holy Christian bottom top side I even put her in the chicken wing giving her dope dick for a good hour trying to beat her back and guts out. I could have fall in love with that holy pussy. This was a one-time thing, I knew this so I beat the brakes off her with every inch I could get in her, she left that motel room with her belly button bruised. I saw her at church one other time I went back to church. She smiled. then turn her head that was the end of that. It's been several girls in the area I've got to beat down a few times, The outlaw dick is what they wanted a shot at, just to know they fuck Joe Roach, The Baddest guy in the county. Trust me, I bless every one of them I got the chance to fuck. If the right one's knew they would hang their head and cry!!

That's been fifteen years ago they don't speak but they still smile as we pass. Their men well let's say husbands now don't have a clue, what a fucking I give those girls. I know they are going to read my books, the ones that don't know, try to figure it out. That's the mission for all of you Christians which four Holy girls was it. I will never tell; God bless me I bless them. Now that was a Blessing. I'll be back in about four years that's what I got left to finish out the ten years I'm serving. I see you at the same church when I get out, until then I'll remember. that smile.

Let's fall back to Tomica in Welch West Va. I lived there with her for about two months. Tomica was fine as fuck and black booty like a mother fucker. It's hard to find back woods black pussy like that these days and time, I have a lot of memories of the good old days Joe Roach being a color-blind outlaw, no one can ever say they lived a life as interesting as I have. They don't make outlaws like me anymore!! Not many people are still living that remember breaking the law the way I did and still alive to write about it. And live every day reliving it in my mind. The good old days pulling off Arm Robberies and getting away with it. As a teenager with a 38-colt nickel plated pearl handle. That gun is still around. That gun is a Legend itself been used by Joe Roach to make a living the best he could.

Joe has been on the wrong side of the law since he was old enough to see over a steering wheel of a vehicle. A lot of people will probably think. there's No way one person could get in to so much. It would be a blessing if that was true. Joe Roach is the biggest outlaw that ever been born in Bedford Co. Even when he's in prison the law men are trying every day to dig up something on him to convict him to keep him in prison. Just as they are right now picking at every word he writes to try use against him to convict him. There's no one hates the sight of a law man the way Joe does. Just so you know, you are allowed. to flip a Law man off, Joe does it all the time. He was arrested one time; The Judge ask the Law man if Joe Curse him? The Law man said with his finger. The Judge ask Joe "did you curse him?" "No" Joe said he Just flip him off as he was passing the Law man on the road driving. When the judge said, "No harm done." That was the maddest I've ever Seen a Law man in my life. This prick flips me off in the courtroom, I smile at him before turn to exit the courtroom. Certain Law men have harassed me most of my life, some has lied to convict me, some are mad simply because I was blessed with a Big dick.

I'm not bragging, I'm just simply telling the truth. So, the ones that don't know me, will know not to listen to the white man's lie's about me on things I've done. They are lying. Even the Law men are so ashamed of their little dick, they lie and take it out on me. The way the Law men and other Haters have fucked me throughout my whole life that's why God didn't give you a big dick. And when I tell you eight inches is small, you best believe you got a baby dick compared to the 11 1/2 from balls to the head that I have, many of the Law men's daughters, wives, mothers and even some grandma done got opportunity to see feel ride the brown worm. Don't Hate the player hate the game. I'm going to drag every Law man I can until the day I die. I encourage everyone to pass the word on for others to buy my books, that way I can afford not to work so I can ride around all day, no matter the cost, I'm going to disrespect every God damn Law man I know by mule dicking their girl. There's no white woman alive that don't want to see a nigger dick on a white man. I'm the only white man that has one of them in color. The brown worm. If you don't know ask somebody or ask me, I'll show you the Brown nigger dick on a white man. That's why I'm the most hated.

Ask anyone that has something to say about me what have I done to them personally? All they can tell you is what they have heard I done, one thing after another over and over. But nothing personally, and if they do, they are the "Haters." Lying to make them look like a victim, we know the only thing they are victim of is the little dick victims, once every one that knows me reads this book.

Remember when you go talking shit from now on about Joe Roach you telling on yourself, you got a little boys dick and you mad. If you had any sense at all, you will not let Joe Roach name come out your mouth. For if you do people will know you got the little dick syndrome. And when you are not around, they going to laugh at your little boy dick. I'm going to break you little dick mother fucker's from talking about Joe Roach, believe that I done figured out the perfect way to call out all you little dick's out. If they were a Hater before they read this book, they really going to be a Hater after they read this book!! I was always a ballsy outlaw what time I wasn't in prison, I have somewhere around fifteen kids maybe more I stop counting at fifteen I know of that many by eight different women. Not the first one I can't go visit any time I like, I must have done something right.

I was fifty years old with a one twenty-year-old girlfriend, she had me a daughter. At the same. time I had a nineteen-year-old mix chick pregnant with twin babies when I got arrested for murder, not long after I was arrested, she had twin little boys their mom's name was Corina. The way Corina and I met was out of the blue. I was at Sheetz looking for Lauren slut of the universe. When I say slut that was really a nice way to put it. I really don't know the words to use, for you to really get the full effect of the kind of girl I'm talking about. Lauren was a lot different than any girl I've ever met in my life. Lauren was the type of girl to always stay in a motel, That's the only place she wanted to stay, she loves every drug she could get her mouth nose or in her arm, a dope Hoe.

LIFE 2

I love the things she would do in bed with men or women she was a trainwreck slut. One dick would piss her off and a dozen would just get her started. She had a pretty who ha and how she kept a who ha so pretty I'll never know. She kept it loaded and getting beat up with every make model and color dick possible twenty-four seven. This type of slut is a freaks dream at the same time a man's pockets nightmare like mine over $300,000 threw away In a years' time doing everything possible in bed and anywhere else.

She could get her clothes off. There was never a time we rented a room with a single bed. It always had to be two beds and they were put together to make one. This was the first thing she done when we move to another motel room because we could only stay in one room for thirty before we had to change room for resident purposes. One thing I can say she was a clean slut after about two hours of ten different size dicks and color dicks beat up every hole she had, she would get up run a tub a water set her cum filled body inside and down in the tub, to soke her who ha and asshole while she washes the rest of her body. A porn star had nothing on this girl. I've never known a girl to know so many men to call and piled up in bed and standing waiting their turn in my whole life. A doorknob has nothing on this slut. There was never a dull moment in the whole year it took us to blow $300,000. Always every drug we wanted was there along with a dealer in four counties including me that was dealing drugs also at this time. I seen times. I'd fall asleep in the chair after being up for a week doing drugs and running train on this slut. Before I fell sleep, I can remember three mule dicks in all three holes she had.

Bottles of dick oil empty laying all over the bed, I woke up, there be ten guys with dicks in her on her of being jack all over her. This is one the truest stories I've ever told. The guys that know Lauren know cause they were there. This slut could never get enough. I'm late getting back one night from going to reup, she runs out of dope. When I get back to the room she's not there, I call her she answers and says let me call you back in fifteen minutes, she calls back in about thirty minutes, saying please come got me, I ask where she was? She said she's not sure let her look around to find out. She calls right back she four fucking counties away. She done took off with five black guys she met at the motel up in Java. They all done took her for some crack all five beat her back front and throat out. I could hear in her voice they done stretch her voice cords in her throat, then put her out at Java store, I told her she was a stupid bitch. Then someone pulls up ask her if she needs a ride. This bitch curses me out tells me to never call her back, takes off with a crack dealer: This is the night I ran Into Corina at Sheetz.

LIFE 2

Corina was riding with a girlfriend when they pulled up to the gas pumps beside me to get gas, Corinas friend tells her to hurry, she had to get back to meet her boyfriend after she drop Corina off. He was going to be pissed off if he found out they been together. On Corina's way back past me, she said nice ride, I was riding a Chrysler 300 purple and black, then she said you should let me drive your car. I said to her she should let me ride that ass, she said really. I said yea she said bet then got her backpack from her friend's car and got in behind the wheel of my 300. When we left Sheetz she ask if I had some dope, just so happen I had Just reup with meth, she smiled when I open the console and showed her a whole pound. Then she said I was her kind of man, then she asks where to? I said you driving you tell me; she said let's get a room. I let her know I already had one In Bedford city Days Inn. She said Days Inn it will be.

She ask ,"what reason I was in Lynchburg. Was my plug in Lynchburg?" "No, I was there looking for the biggest slut in the world." She said "don't tell me you must be talking about Lauren." I didn't have to answer she knew exactly who I was looking for when I said the biggest slut of the universe, she said she know Lauren, Lauren was the most dick taking girl she had ever know, we quickly got off that conversation. Corina was a nineteen-year-old pretty mix Chick; she made it no secret she like rolling the bubble smoking meth. And she was game for about anything when it comes to sex, she said one thing about her she was nothing like Lauren. I ended up having twin boys by Corina, her sister has the boys, Corina was arrested in Ohio for a murder overdose. Her and her friend went there to get drugs. Got fentanyl instead the drug they paid for. Her friend was dead minutes after they scored the dope, sitting in the front seat behind the wheel of her own car. Corina young she admitted to purchasing the dope for her and her friend, she ends up with five years. I gave custody to her sister of the twins, after giving up custody to her sister with a verbal agreement that she stay in touch I've not seen the twins since that day.

I'm sure they are doing fine, Tracie their aunt could never have children, she always wanted children, she was going through a divorce at this time, I'm shore having these twins in her life took up a lot of her time and help her get through her divorce. At least I know with her they have a promise future. As long as they don't have a criminal mind like their Daddy. Tracie has never been one to do drugs always had a good life, I feel like I done the right thing for the twins. What I got to offer is only a big setback in any child's life, when you have every Lawman in the state out to get you like I do. That's not future for any child. Like about the stupidest dumbest person alive I got back with Lauren before I sign the custody papers, Lauren tried to get me not to give custody to Tracie, she wanted us to raise the twins, with a promise she would change. It's no way I would take that chance. I feel like even if I don't see them again, they are in the best care they could ever be in. I think it all turned out to be a blessing for the twins and Tracie.

Of course, Lauren and I are not together, she did not get her shit together, being even more of a slut than she ever was. How that could be possible you would have figure that out on your own, I finally left that slut alone. I wish I knew then what I know now, after $300,000 that should open anyone's eyes. Not many people have money like that to throw away. I still feel like the lucky one I got away from her. She has no respect for herself. From what I hear that has not changed, my life was much better when I finally got away from her. It took ten years in prison for that to happen. Even though I spent ten years there, that turned out to be a blessing. While doing that ten year's I learn a lot about something I never care to learn about. That was God how I come about my first bible while I was in prison is a crazy story, I started out by reading the Old Testament the King James Bible. Not turning to God because I was in prison like so many claims to do, I read the Bible in my cell. by myself because I was curious. How I come about this king James bible, most people would not tell.

This King James Bible was about the nicest Bible I had ever seen before. It had to be expensive red leather with bold gold letters that said King James bible on the front. It showed up in a poker game. I was running in prison, The hand that was being wild card hand I like playing I played about every time it was my turn to deal. I wanted this Bible for what reason I do not know. It was something inside of me that said I want that, Bible. It was my turn to deal; I called the game Jack and your low black my favorite hand of poker I'd came up with. I was pretty good with the cards making sure always the first card I dealt me was Jack that was the fourth card in the deck.

Then I made sure the Bottom card was a Jack after the first Jack was dell then! delt me the second one from the bottom very quickly so wasn't caught me cheating. It was a five-card hand with the next three that I got, when you are playing wild cards its always going to be five of a kind about 90% of the time I had five As that's how I won that Bible. I've never lived by the Lord, I read a lot and learn a lot about God. It's really a lot easier to live by the Lord than to live the everyday life in the world today. The devil has so much play in the world today you might think you doing a good deed, the whole time it's the devil's work, being done by the devil himself making bad things look so good. Thats how easily God's people are being misled and confused.

LIFE 2

The devil not a living creator, the devil is in anything that's evil. The devil can make your day so bad you just throw your hands up. That's the test we are put through every day. Either throw your hands up and let the Devil win and that's the easiest thing to do. Go to work for the devil, doing bad is always easier. The devil shows you a big pot of gold that's on the other side of his rainbow. The more bad you do the closer you get to that pot of gold. That pot is the biggest pot you have ever seen. You got have that, so you do even more bad to get there faster, when you get there inside that pot is no gold, it's the lake of fire you work so hard for now you are finally there, his mission is accomplish, "next". My favorite person in the Bible was Job he reminded me 'so much of my daddy, My dad has never known much about religion, But I think he was a man like Job, a man after Gods heart, He does not believe in lying, stealing or anything other than being a good man working hard to get what he wants. Him and my mom raise six of us, I got two brothers and three sisters.

My baby sister is my favorite sister, then there's my oldest sister she next to my favorite, then there's my middle sister, she can't stand me, plus she's a lawyer what should I expect. The Bible will tell what chance a Lawyer has in getting to heaven, about like the chance a camel has of getting threw the eye of a needle. I love my sister that's something she's got to deal with, It's no need in trying to plead with God about this he said what he said and its wrote in the Bible. What you trying to say he's a liar!! I'm just saying I read the Bible that's all. Don't hate me for telling the truth, like so many of you already do because I speak the truth. My brother Jeremy is the baby of the litter, he's everybody's favorite. He's mine and Jody's, that's my favorite sister's name. My older brother Jerry he's a hard worker. Came a long way for himself thinking about himself. Thats paid off for him.

As for me being kindhearted and giving anyone the shirt off my back. Has done nothing for me but allow the rest to run over me then when I finally act pissed off, something is the matter with me. They were so used to treating me like that and when I got pissed off, I wasn't acting right. So, half my life I acted right and was treated like shit. The other half when I didn't act right. They wanted nothing to do with me. I know for a fact I have been cut from the family tree that's been made sure of by the lawyer of the family. My mom has been as good to me as she's been allowed to be by others in the family that has control issues, If she does do anything for me I'm told I better not let the other's find out or she want help me anymore. My dad he's done figured out if he was going to be left alone so he could live in peace he had to limit what he does for me. My dad has been a wonderful dad If you ever want to know what kind of man my daddy has been read Job in the

Bible. I've never turned my life over to God. It's sad that I haven't as much as I know about God, with being a Christian I can say I've probably forgot more than most will ever know about the one's I feel like should worry as the one thing I was raised just not knowing anything about God.

All my family say I'm going to Hell. I don't know what God's going to do with me. I'm not really worried about going to Hell. I feel like I've lived In Hell most of my life. The ones that should worry are the ones that don't know what I do know. People have always been quick to judge my life, never have they taken the blinders off their eyes to see how their own has really turn out. All I'm saying is you need to make sure what pot of gold you are living for. I'm not trying to doubt anyone's life or judge, I'm just saying don't be so disheartened when it doesn't turn out like you expect it to. All I can do is look for the worst and hope for the best, cause I know I've been judged already by everyone but the one that matters. Thats the only shot I got. The Bible says there will be no favors!!!

I've never claim to be a godly person, I've done more than my share wrong. Not like everyone else God hasn't seen only the wrong I've done, He knows the good I got in in my heart and soul that goes a long way, what no one else wants to see he sees in me every day. The Bible says don't worry about tomorrow, live for today because none of us are promise tomorrow. I'm not going to say Lauren is a bad person, she's just been lead like me down the wrong path for what reason I don't know. She's a pretty girl but that lifestyle is not for me. It took me $300,000 and ten years in prison to figure that out. I have seen more peace in prison than I did living that lifestyle. At least I don't have to worry or be stressed out. At any time be charge with drugs maybe even prostitution, for the money I spent. For everybody else it was free, no matter how good I was to someone. I think it there is such a thing that there are people born with a future and there are others born without one. I've made a lot of bad decisions, most the time they come behind there were no other options. Some people think everyone has a choice in life, that's not true. I was not the one to choose a life without a future. That was chosen for me, by so many that made sure I never stood a chance, it all started in the messed-up place I was raise Roachtown.

When you have certain family members that would make life Hell for my family, because they didn't like me even as a little boy. In other family members' eyes, I never deserved anything. And for my parents to do for me even as a kid, they would be outcasted for it. Others in my family made me out to be nothing but a liar and anything else they I felt I should be, I was one miserable kid growing up in Roachtown. It seems like every day

LIFE 2

if anyone had a bad day they Just stop by our house and tell something. Whether I had done it or not, I get the Hell beat out of me right there in front of them. There's still a lot more love in my heart than should be. I know I'd never been treated that way by my mom and dad- the way I was treated if it wasn't for all the others that treat me like shit every day of my childhood growing up. People don't think about this until the time comes. Especially the one's on their death bed. There's only hand full of people in Roachtown that's not going to think about what they done to me on their death bed, you will take it grave, every damn one of you are going to pay dearly, believe that and all of you know that. Thats when I get still alive my pleasure in knowing you are getting back what you give. Good luck u all going to need it as you can lie to the world but you can't lie to God!!!

Have you ever heard of a Godly outlaw? There's a lot of things in my life I've heard of and never seen before. I got to be one these types of outlaws. There's no way I could have got away with as much as I've got away with without God's help. Just like the time I stuck that 38 colt in the cashier's face and demanded the money. That was the devil's work. Then again God help things go as well as I plan by making sure the lady put all the money in the bag. God works in many ways. That's like the trips from Texas with the Mexicans. Even though what I was doing was illegal.

God knew I didn't mean no harm. The Mexicans wanted to better their self by the United States. The land of the free, why is it they not allowed. God did not say that the law did. Thats why laws are made to be broken. Sometimes it takes outlaws like me to do God's work, God could have at any time had me pulled over search and thrown in prison. The reason God didn't there was more good being done than harm.

The Mexicans got to better their self. And I got paid to help them do so, therefore for God seen that as a good deed. If not, I'd probably still be in prison as human trafficking is a serious crime. Just like when I robbed the northerner contractors, the south built that lake to help build the state and communities, the lake surrounded. The lake was built to support the counties it was built by the south. This was going to happen regardless of the north, we allowed them to buy the lake property. Just because we allow you to do something don't mean you can put us out. The north had the game twisted, God stood behind me while got them lined out. If they were doing nothing wrong God has the power to make sure my mission wasn't accomplished. My mission was accomplished without the first problem. What does that tell you? I could have never done this with God's help.

If you don't like our God carry your ass back up north, you better ask somebody. When the world realize God loves everybody then we might be able to live together. Money is a lot of people's God and they will perish first. If you know God so well, why do we all second guess everything we hear, except what you hear about me of course? Well enough about something I know nothing about. I'm just an outlaw making up my own religion as I go along. You know I can do that cause I'm Joe Roach. The Legends of all Legends in the south. If I can't break the law, It can't be broke, And if I can't make up the laws to satisfy me they can't be made up. Remember this is my book

Chapter 4 My Religion

My name is Joe Roach. I don't know much about religion,
The first time I seen the inside of a church, I was in my twenties I
wasn't there for Sunday services, I was there for a funeral. I'm not
sure who it was that past, my dad told me I needed to come to
show my respects to the family. So, I did cause my dad told me to.
It had to be a family member. That didn't mean shit to me,
probably was one the Hater's you know every family has them.
Our family seems to have more than most families. I know this
because most of my family are some shit. There's not many that I
care about, I'm going to name them. If you don't see your name on
this list, you know how I feel about you, it's no secret you a piece
of shit. If your name is not on this list do not show up at my
funeral. And if you do, I'm going to roll over and shit in your face.

Here's the list:
God
The rest you Haters can continue doing what you are doing
and be a Hater and go to Hell. I've never seen shit piled so high in
one family. I'm sorry this story had to start off so blunt and to the

point. If you had to live life the way I have you would feel the same way if truth was told all you have family you feel this way about. This story is going to be different than any story I've ever written. This is going to be about a person not many of you know. Get to know Joe Roach, you might see him differently than what you hear about him.

What did Jesus say to the people that wanted to stone the slut to death? The one without sin cast the first stone. These people that wanted to kill this slut, were really good people. At least they were honest enough to themselves to know they were sinners. They pitched the stone to the ground and walked away. In today's world they would have stone that slut to death. Not only are they sinner's they liars to their self and to Jesus nowadays. Back in those days they had faith and belief. They knew Jesus knew they all were sinner's and would be held responsible if they cast a stone and delt with. I read the whole Bible throughout the time I was locked up for all these years, I done my reading at night, where it was just me and God. Not that I was ashamed of reading the Bible. I wasn't ready to commit to something I knew nothing about. Then I had to hear the dumbest shit every day from guys in prison trying to convince themselves they have a good girl on the street.

Thats something I never done was brag on a girl while I was locked up. Even in the Bible I read about how shady women was to their husbands while their husband at war fighting; women getting pregnant by other men even the king while their husband was out risking life for a king who was sleeping with his wife. If a woman will do that to her husband, don't tell me what a good woman you got while prison, you got to be the biggest, joke I know. 80% of the men locked up are locked up behind a woman, I can honestly say I've never been locked up behind a woman.

And the guys that were, were always saying what a good woman they had. Truth is the truth, every woman I know that had a man in jail was glad he was in jail. By time he got out to go back with a woman after serving time in prison, you just asking to go back to prison. If she had so many dicks sticking out of her as she had in her while you were locked up she would look like a porcupine, That's how I feel about all good women while their husband or boyfriend been in prison.

I may be wrong if I am the Bible is lying. You tell me what would you believe? I've never really tried to build a relationship with any girl I'd been with after I got out of prison, even my baby's mom when I loved her the whole time I was in prison. We stayed in touch for the kids. For some time, I thought about us getting back together. After ten years that's all it was, a thought. Over the years' time changes everybody heart, even when you together for so long it changes, There's no way any woman can say she loves you after ten year's being away from you. Nothing will be the same, you best believe that. My baby's mama both will agree on that. The Bible doesn't lie, from what I read of it. Thats front to back, everything I've read I Can say I've either seen similar things or similar things are still happening. Just like it says is going to happen every day. The Bible plays out like it wrote every day.

I'm not just dogging women out; men are some shit. When a girl's boyfriend sits out in my driveway while his girl crawls through my bedroom window because I'm sleep didn't hear her beat on the door even if she beat on the door. She crawls in my bedroom window gives me head and whatever else I want just for a $20 piece of dope. After we are done, she does the dope and nods out naked in the bed, minutes later her man's knocking on the door, I let him in give him a $50 worth dope to take her with him. Here take her clothes with you. He's not mad after he gets some dope. That's the kind of men that's taking care of the women these days. Who's really taking care of who? Thats the power of dope mainly heroin and Fentanyl the world is strung out on. I've done a lot of things in my lifetime, but never have I done heroin or Fentanyl. Thats a promise death to whoever does do it. People want to blame me for selling drugs. If they don't get it from me, they are going to get it from somebody, you best believe that. What I do not understand about people these days is if I see some one that just got killed over, I surely wouldn't ask for the same thing that person got. If a dopehead see someone dead, they say they want the same drug that one got. That's how strung-out people are now. Me myself see someone dead I don't want no parts of whatever they took.

These people now say let me get the same thing, plus let me get a $50 piece extra they will take the dead person with them. Bet here's a fifty get rid of the dead person. What I'm about to tell you is mind blowing. They drag the corpse to the car, ride the corpse around until they run out of dope, then they take their needle and drain the corpse. Shooting up their blood to get high from the drug that's in the dead corpse/system, the reason it doesn't kill them is because the body has broken it down to a level to get high after draining the corpse they throw the corpse out. They call that a dry corpse when it's found with a drop of blood left in the body. If you think I'm crazy Google it "dry corpse." Thats how bad the fem's have got in today's world doing Fentanyl. Very sad to know what a dopehead will do to your child just to get high sad but true. If you have any loved one's strung out on heroin its most likely going to be Fentanyl that's going to kill them, and to find them this way is very likely this day and time "dry corpse." How do I know about this? In the dope world you live and learn.

LIFE 2

This is a message that this can and will happen to if you do Fentanyl. This drug has no friends and takes no hostages. With Fentanyl Its a promise death. If you are a drug dealer selling heroin you are selling Fentanyl, so don't think saying you didn't know is going to get you off. When the Law comes to get you out, they are going to smoke you. Thats not a warning, that's a promise. Just know it's not worth it. People die every day, and you know what you are doing to a lot of people that don't know what they are doing. Fentanyl.

I hope I've never sold anyone drugs that kill someone. I do not know of any. After all I've heard and seen, never again will I take a chance to be blamed for anyone that does heroin and Fentanyl is not the way to make a living. The only thing you are going to get is a lifetime in prison, and many loved one's dead. Take some hard advice sell any drug you want, just not heroin or Fentanyl. If you think you got all the sense, keep selling Fentanyl and when one day ends your day is going to end with it. The Law is going to put their foot down. I can say I hate a Law man. This drug Fentanyl I support the Law 100%, fuck Fentanyl. If you in it to win it, I'd rather be left out of it, it's out of control.

Following God is hard if you have never done it before, No one in this world is perfect, A lot of people say I'm a Bad person. I'm sure I could be a better person than I have been. At the same time, I do not think I've been really as bad as I've been made out to be. I'm sure God is disappointed with me. As many times as he saved my life, it always seemed like I'd smack him in his face, when I didn't need him anymore. Don't get me wrong I never got into anything then ask God to help me. I am a firm believer if I didn't need help getting into something, getting out of it is something I would have to do by myself. God knows his self whether you're worth saving or not. And what other people thinks doesn't amount to a hill of beans, to how God feels. People say you can be helped only so much. In real life that's so true. After being helped over and over and over people eventually give up on you. Sometimes "helping you" and "helping you" are two different things.

Helping someone get well or get over a death or get on their feet when they are brokenhearted and lost is the kind of help God's looking to see, hear and feel. Thats the help of a real friend. To help someone with money instead of love a lot of times is No help at all, It may feel like you have done a good deed, and you may have intended to be doing a good deed. Money has never fixed anything. In God's eyes, money is the root of all evil. Anything money can get you out of has a catch to it in the end. After over $250,000 in lawyer fees threw out twenty-five throughout my life, and around twenty-five years spent in prison, that goes to show money is not the answer. If it was, I wouldn't still be in prison with four more years left to finish out another ten years.

My Dad is one of the greatest men that I will ever know. As long as he was footing the bill I stayed in trouble, no matter if he could get me out or not. The money him, my mom and baby sister Jody would spend on me in prison, made It like I was on a vacation rather than learning a lesson for having done wrong. These three people ore the most important people in my life. Not only my mom and dad but my baby sister has spent every dollar she ever made to make sure I lived good even though I was in prison. A lot of people will never know how easy I have had it my whole life. Not until now I look back and see what a life wasted. Spoiled is not the word I'm looking for. Being able to live good and doing good are two different things. It's all in what way you are l looking at doing good. Learning from your mistakes and trying to better yourself by knowing not make the same mistake twice or doing good in a way that you don't learn anything a lot like I've done most of my life, I'll explain a little more in detail that way you can get a better picture of what I'm saying.

Money to most people is good, money can do just about anything. I'm living proof of that even if it can't buy me out of everything, I didn't care because I knew even though I was in prison I would live good either way. Prison was sometimes a break I needed, not that it got me on the right path, I was never the type to take responsibility for anything I did, I've always had a twisted reason for what I'd done to get in prison, whatever reason satisfied me. Thats all that matter for me to know in my mind I done no wrong. Doing time was the easy part. Especially with the way my mind works, one thing I knew when I got in trouble, the life I lived on the outside was dead to me. It was the life I lived in prison, was the only thing that matter. How easy and how I spent my time was up to me, I always chase the simple prison life. "Go with it" live as comfortable as I could. I can do bad no matter where I'm at. As long as I got money, I Could always make happen whatever I wanted to happen. This was not something God would ever approve of. When you are the person, I've been throughout my life. It didn't matter what God like it was all about me and what made me happy. That was the selfishness that lived inside me. I'm smart enough to know there's three ways to live in this world. There's the easy way the right way and the wrong way. The easy way is mostly the wrong way. Thats mostly the lifestyle I've been living. I'm not proud of it but at the same time it's not been a bad way to live, especially in prison, if you look at it in my perspective, but in God's eye's it's the right way or nothing good could come out of it. I do know that much about the life I'm living. When this is all you know, this is the way you adjust to living. It all boils down to the kind of money you can get your hands on that shows how you can live in prison, as well as it does when you are not in prison. The devil is a powerful person. You never know what part the devil is going to play from day to day. One day the devil Can be your worst enemy, the next day the devil can be your bests friend. The devil can be many genders in here or out there no matter where you at. As long as you leave the door open the devil will come in.

Your way of living is on you. The devil makes it look much easier to live the devil's way. The reason I don't make the devil out to be a man or a woman is because the devil can be whoever the devil chooses and whatever it takes for you to live the devil's way. The devil will be whoever it takes to make sure it plays out in the devil's favor. The devil can be a good honest man or he can be a beautiful woman, It does not matter to the devil. Tricks are for kids and we are all kids when it comes to the devil playing tricks. We are a lot of times the devil our self, doing the work for the devil, I've been around the devil a lot in my life. As long as you doing the wrong things in life the devil is your best friend. The one thing you do right the devil is mad. God is a selfish God. God has every right to be, if you look at all God has done that the devil is taking all the credit for. It all boils down to the respect we give. That's something a lot of us don't have. We don't respect our self how can we respect God or anyone else. The devil doesn't require no respect. As long as the devil can keep you doing bad that's all the respect the devil needs. The saying we can do bad all by yourself, is a true statement. We could also do good if we wanted to. You can do one just as easy as the other. The devil just makes bad look a lot easier than good a lot of the time in our eyes. Tricks are for kids a lot of us are being tricked one way or another every day and we continue to go along with the devil and the devil's trick's it just so much easier for one simple reason: it's more fun in doing bad than good, especially when your heart has been hardened by the devil. What is so sad it's like throwing a stick in the path of a mentally challenged man, woman or child to watch them fall down, then laugh cause it's so funny to hurt someone. They live a life of danger every day, and don't know no better.

That's how sad and sick the world has become. I do believe in karma. What makes you laugh now will make you cry later. Those men, women or children were put here to test our love, not to be made fun of. When you trick them, they don't know, they only know love. You are making a fool out of yourself. I'd like to ask one question: How many of these special men women or children have you ever seen, without a smile on their face if you smile at them? Their heart is full of love, something a lot of us will never know how It really feels to have the love in our heart the way they do, and the love they share every day waking up in the wicked and cruel world we are making for them, sad but true.

I have an nephew with down syndrome, his mom is my oldest sister Jenny, his name is Gab. At two months old he had open heart surgery. He was cut down the middle laid open then put back together again. When he was in recovery, as soon as his eyes opened, what did he do? He smiled laying there strapped to a little bed, staples from his throat pretty much to his belly button where had been opened up, then put back together. He smiles without a care in this world, looking to be more painful than any normal person could bare, He smiles as if he didn't care as if there was no pain. That's God's way of telling us love don't hurt. After he smiled to let my sister know he was ok, He went back to sleep. My sister never left his side. Every couple of hours he would open his eyes to make share she was still there. He would smile then close his eyes again. How could anyone hurt a child like this? And if you do God is going to punish you. All Gab will have his whole life is his mama. God could have never picked a better mama than my sister Jenny to raise a more loving child than Gab.

Here's a perfect example of a mama's love. You will know what I'm talking about if you were raised on a farm like we all were. When a cow has a calf, try to walk up and pet it. Trust me you don't want to do that, because mama is not going to act right at all. You will find out about a mother's love, you not going to get close to that calf believe that. And if you don't believe me, try it see how it works out for you. This is the same kind of love my sister has for Gab, only a mama knows that kind of love, that's not just a sometime love for a child, that's a love that last a lifetime. I want my sister Jenny to know she's not only been a great sister, but she's also the greatest when it comes to being a mother and especially Gabs mama. Keep up the good work. The only place you can go when your work is done, you done earn your seat in Heaven. Can't nobody take that seat from you nor can anyone else walk one step in your shoes. That's really what a great person you are. Jenny, the reason I put you in my book is because I want everybody know you are a wonderful and great person, but never as wonderful and great as my sister Jody but you already knew that, as for you Judy don't take these words to heart, I know what I'm about to say is going to break your heart. Even though you have never liked me, you have made that clear to me many times, I know I've been a brother that's been hard to love, especially when you don't have a heart big enough to love everybody. I knew I'd be the first cut from the family tree. I just want you to know the truth how I feel about you. I love you with all my heart. You a great sister great mom a great wife to your great husband. Just wanted you to know my heart's never been as cold as the picture I sometimes made it out to be. Now that's said at the end of the day it's not what you give it's how you feel, you are love by your brother Joe forever if that's not a good thing all I can say is get over it. It is what it is.

Back to the life of Joe Roach in and out of prison, And why he never really never learn a lesson, I really boils down to his mom, dad and sister Jody, making sure he never done without anything, you would think as much drugs I had going on when I wasn't in prison, I'd be doing drugs or in some way have something to do with drugs going on while I was in prison. I've never done the first drug while I was in prison. That was one thing I made sure I didn't get into. I took the money my family sent me and got into everything else that was illegal to do in prison. Of course, no matter what prison I was in, there's always some that works there got put on my dad's payroll. Like you have read in book one called life and in book two called life two, someone being on payroll got started as far back as the boy's home with a couple staff one name Karen another name Sandra. Both young ladies were black ladies that work at the boy's home. Sandra, I met my first stay at the home boy's home,

On my next stay I was a little older, so I was at another boy's home in Richmond Va. Her name was Karen, back then in the middle eighties $500 a month was enough to pay rent light bill and car payment, that's how much things have changed over the year's right now it's 2024. It was a big difference from then and now. We will get to all that. Even as a teenager I'm the one to blame or was it the ladies that were responsible for me at the time, teaching me to do the wrong things. My mom and dad were just making sure their son was safe and being watch over, by women that were much older, being paid to be a mother figure, while I was in the boy's home that way my mom and dad knew I was safe. The black ladies and I were at a different perspective. That worked out greatly in my favor. All that was really expected of them was to make sure I got a carton of cig each week. Cig was only $20 carton back then. That was $80 a month, what was the other $420 for? That was so moms and dad knew I was safe. I was as safe, spoiled and everything else a sixteen- & seventeen-year-old teenager could be! I was good in every way I could be given the situation I was in. To me I was in a good situation, I didn't miss being out at all really. By reading my books you can tell by my first stay in the boy's home, I wasn't out long I was back to finish out my juvenile life the same way. Was I to blame or was it the devil's work? I think now looking back even though I was underage played part in what was going on. What the women and I both were doing the devil's work; I was good with that!

After reading some of David in the King James Bible I dream the craziest dream's it was kind of about the Bible. It was like I was fighting a battle like was talk about in the Bible, except while everyone was fighting each other with swords. I was running from a dragon. Every time I'd hide behind a tree it would fly over and breathe fire on the tree and the tree would turn to ashes in front of me, I'd run find another tree to hide behind another tree, the dragon would circle come right back do the same thing. I got up on a rooftop as I tried to clime the pottery shingles spin out from under my feet. I finally made it to the chimney. I was able to hide by keep circling around the chimney. Finally, the dragon flew away. Everyone on the ground was still fighting, bodies lying everywhere. Then I woke up breathing hard the dream was so real I said to myself I better leave that Bible alone If it was going to make me dream crazy dreams like the one I Just had. I left the Bible alone for about a week. Then one night around twelve I couldn't sleep, I got it out of my box, started reading where I left off. I'm not a fast reader and this Bible had the middle column to help understand words I couldn't make out what they were saying. That helped me a lot. I read on through the night until came time the next morning to eat breakfast, then I laid down. I was tired so it didn't take long I was asleep, Then I started to dream again. This time it was no dragon It was a lot of fighting killing Just like it was in movies I'd watch about back in those days, I'm Interested even more about this book, The dreams Stop for a while, then when I got to Job the dream came back. Job is my favorite of all in the Bible, Job reminds me of my dad and all his struggles to get what he got in life. I dream about Job from the beginning to the end.

Job was afraid of God and turn his head away from the devil. He had a lot of sons, a few daughters and a lot of livestock. He had a lot of slaves. His slaves were not treated like slaves they were treated like Job wanted to be treated, everyone was very respectable. Job's sons would throw a party and invited their sisters to party with them. Job knew they were doing things they shouldn't be doing. What was wrong in God's eyes was wrong in Job's eyes, but these were his children. He loved each and every one of them. After their wild party he would send for them, knowing they all had sin, he knew they had wrong God, him and their self. He sacrificed offerings for them to God hoping God would forgive them for their sins.

Then come a day the devil said to God, "why do you make over Job the way you do?" God said to the devil, "Job is one the most loyal man I know." The devil said, "yes I'd be a loyal man to if you handed me everything, I Ever wanted like you do Job." God told the devil "You could never be a loyal man, that's why you got casted cut of Heaven, for trying to stab me in the back. That's why you are not worthy to put a foot in Job's shoes. Job's a loyal and blameless man." The devil said to God "take away all he has; he will curse you to your face!" The devil could see he was setting up God in a way only the devil can do and to the devil he was the only one could with this get away with this. And he knew what he was doing he was picking at God to get his way to make trouble for Job.

Sure, enough he got what he wanted. God told the devil, "Ok show me you can make Job curse me, but you better not kill Job." So, the devil set out to do what he loved to destroy people's lives. Jobs sons had invited their sisters over for a feast and party, like they always done. The devil had their house flattened killing all Job's son's and daughter's. Then the devil had all Job's slaves killed all but a few they were left alive so they could tell Job what the devil had done, plus the devil had all his oxen and donkey stole from him also. After all this bad news at one time Job fell to his knees and prayed to God. Job thanked God for all he had gave him over the years, then he praised God. Never did Job say a curse word.

The devil went back to see God, God said "you tried to get Job to turn on me without reason you done what you done. But still Job did not curse God." The devil said, "he will curse you." So, the devil went back to earth to pay Job another visit. Not that he hadn't already punished Job enough. The devil took another try at Job striking him with boils all over his body from head to feet. Job set out by a pile of ashes with a piece of glass and scraped himself with the glass and cover his self in ashes to keep from getting infected sores. Job's wife said, "Are you loyal and honor God now look at all He's done you should curse God and die." Job said "You act just like a crazy woman. When God was giving you was happy and continue to accept the life He gave us. But when trouble comes your way, you quickly change and blame God. If you want to curse God and die you go ahead. Job is going to worship and honor God with pride and ask Him for forgiveness. Never did Job ever say a harsh word to God. When it was all said and done God blessed Job with Ten times more than he had before. Job lived about 400 years. Now this is my version of Job. It's been twenty years since I read about Job. I'm writing this book solely on what I read and learn over my lifetime.

So, if you read somethings that don't sound right just know I tried and I'm not a Christian but I do believe in Jesus Christ, God and all the good that He's done for me, I believe He still believes in me, one day I'll get it right. I have never been one to turn to him in prison. He gave me a lot of chances to find Him or ask Him to come into my life. I feel prison is not where I want to start asking for someone I really never knew. I do know I owe him a lot. If it wasn't for God it's no way I'd be still alive, It's been some miracles in my life. When I say miracles, I mean life or death miracles I would have never survive without him. That's how serious things. Were wrong in being was at times in my life. Being shot and survive wasn't a miracle I was just lucky, even though one bullet across my muscle of my left chest and, I graze my left nipple and lodge into the muscle my left arm. I consider that being lucky. Miracle was when I was poison with battery acid a to kill me, I laid in a coma for more than three weeks, my family was called in twice to discuss unplugging me. My sister Jody said give another week, me and my wife at the time were not together. There was a $100,000 life insurance policy in her name at the time. She comes in, my baby mama was there with me as my family ask her to be there. She's always loved me, and she needed to be there. She probably the only woman that love me besides Missy. Missy we will talk about later. She was my ride or die girl our life was interesting, for now let's get back to me laying in a coma. Donna was my baby mama. She left out so my wife could spent a moment alone with me. When she came back my wife was gone and I was unplugged. Thats when I was moved to p.c. in the hospital. Donna was the only one allowed in the room, beside my mom and Jody my sister. A couple days before I was going to be unplugged, I came out of a coma, Donna was asleep in the bed with me when I woke up. At first, I didn't know who she was, I didn't know nobody not even my mom. The doctor told my mom I had enough battery acid to kill an elephant in my system. That came from someone giving me poison crystal meth, me in a coma and being unplug by my wife, me coming out of a few days before I was going to be unplug was a miracle. God had something else in store for me. I didn't ask him to save me, but I'm glad he did. Why He did I still don't know. What's sad. about this miracle that he made happen. As Soon as I got well, I smacked him in the face again. Thats how ungrateful I was. Back doing the same thing.

Chapter 5 My Real-Life Ghost Story Experience

Not long after I was out the hospital, I met a lady the house she lived in turns out has a ghost there also. This ghost was a little boy that was the son of one my cousins. He burn up in a house fire, and this house was the only place he felt safe. It was his grandma's house across the road from the house he burn up in. He loved his grandma. This is where his spirit came after his death came much too early. This is one of those story's that can't be made up, my cousin, his father so I guess that makes him my cousin too. Him and his wife were getting a divorce. His wife had four other children by other men, my cousin stayed a lot with his grandma that lived across the road upon the hill located on Old Woman's Creek Brights Va. The house the boy lived in when he was born was a small log cabin located on the opposite side of the road then the little boy's grandmother lived on Old Woman's Creek Brights Va. The boy was with his grandma a lot, she loved him like most grandmas do unconditionally this little boy loved his grandma the same way, my cousin the little boy's daddy him and the boy's mom were separated, going through the courts over custody of the little boy.

The little boy's daddy, my cousin, won custody of his son. The Judge orders the little boy's mom to turn the little boy over to his daddy the next morning at the courthouse. That night the little boy burns up in a house fire. The mother gets out the other four children to safety. This little boy is the only one left behind. There's a lot of stories about that night. Some say the little boy's remains were found in a closet area and the closet latch was found locked along with the little boy's remains. I only can tell the stories I hear. It's awfully funny the little boy was the only one that didn't make it out!

Some year's later I met a girl that lived in the little boy's grandma's house it was a cider side Ranch house with a inground pool. That little boy made his way around that house real good, I don't think the house was haunted I think that's where the little boy was loved at the most and that's where he lived after being burn to death in his mother's house across the road. I remember lying on the bed in the master bedroom. I could feel the mattress move on both sides often as if the little baby was playing hopping back and forward over me. I see shadows of the little boy all the time. He was always moving around in the house. One morning I got up to put my boots on there was something in my boots. I put my hand in and pulled it out it was toilet paper pack in my boot perfectly formed to make the boot's size much smaller. The other one was the same way. That day was the last I seen of that little boys shadows, sometimes before that day you could tell he had been playing in the big swimming pool, cause there be water around it at different places where he been jumping in and getting out. It had to be the little boy cause all the times this happen, no one was around that day me and my girl were at work and this is about we would find when we got home. The day the bag was in my boots I think I found peace for the little boy. The old shack he burn up in still stood more than half burn across the road. The little boy's great uncle owns the land and old burn shack at this time. He asks me one day what I charge to take it the rest of the way down burn it do whatever I had to get rid of it as it was an eye sore and bad memories Just to look at it. I gave him a price he gives me the go ahead I tear it down salvage what logs could be salvaged to take to the Roach Ranch. After clearing the burnt cabin, I never saw the shadows no more.

Chapter 6 Prison Life

The last years of my prison life. I understand more every day why the jails and prisons are overcrowded. I'm at Flatland prison. Out of fifteen hundred, inmates fourteen hundred and ninety are strung out on suboxone strips. I've seen fiends before but never have I seen so many people strung out behind something that isn't even a drug. You know it's real bad when someone is sent to prison because of drugs, you think there's no better place to get clean than prison, prison is supposed to be the place you will get clean from drugs one way or another. That use to be a promise from the Department of Corrections. Now if you want to get high go to prison. The Department of Corrections offers a drug program that promise you will be strung out like a lab rat every day you in prison up until the day you are release, you will walk out of prison even more strung out than you were when you got to prison. This is one reason the crime rate is so high as you have more people trying to get in prison than get out. When you a dopehead you don't have it as good as you do in prison.

Out there unless you are dealing, most dope head's wake up sick, Thats when they do whatever it takes to get it, don't question what a dopehead lab rat will do for a piece of dope out there or in prison. It's much easier to get it in prison, you just sign up for the drug program. The staff bring the drug to you three times a day. To make sure you stay strung out like lab rat. That's job security for the staff that work the drug program. You would think in this program you would have to attend classes about drug abuse. Not here you just get more going to strung out three times a day. They going to bring it to you. One thing about the state Department of Corrections, they know how to rob the federal government. Reminds me of the eighties when we were robbing the feds for kilos of cocaine. They were bringing into Miami by the tons to use for job security their self.

The state is using these drug programs in the Department of Corrections to do the same thing, job security, no matter how bad they get the inmates strung out. As long as the federal government keeps paying for the drug program, the more the state will keep the state inmates looking like lab rats. It's all about that money. Who better than a junky lab rat strung out on free dope to lie about how the program saves their life. A dopehead will say whatever needs to be said for dope. You know if Inmates suck dick for quarter strip, they wouldn't mind lying for a whole one. This is how strung out the state Department of Corrections have the inmates that like to get high looking like lab rats. Even collapsing on the sidewalk.

This is the way time is being served in state prison. The federal government is paying for it! This is a field I can talk about. Not the first time I ever got high in prison. I'm not in prison behind drugs nor am in prison for telling. I sit back in my cell watching everything going on around me. Then I write about prison life. I have never been so happy as I was the morning the C.O. called my name, Roach, "pack your shit you being transferred first thing the next morning."

I did not know where I was going, I did not care where I was going. Just as long as I was leaving that Hellhole! Being there you knew as soon you got there as a white inmate that was a black run prison, black inmates done and said whatever they wanted to the black staff. If you were white you best stay in your cell, the first opportunity a black staff got they would write your cracker ass a charge. At this prison it was hard time for the white man. My first night there I slept on a metal bed no mattress. I'd ask several times throughout the day. The black staff said don't ask no more if you do you want get a mattress. The next day another shift came on and they were still pricks about giving me a mat. They did all this treatment came behind being white. It was hard for the white man to get a shower at that prison where 98% of the C.O's were females and black. If you know anything about blacks they all brothers and sisters and they going to look out for each other,

LIFE 2

This is how it works in prison, you put two black inmates together as celly's within a few days they going to be fucking and sucking each other. Put a black and a white together to be celly's, if the white guy don't let the black guy fuck him, the white guy is racist. The black guy is going to cause trouble for his white racist celly because he won't let him fuck him in the ass!!! When you see two blacks as celly's they fucking. When you see a black and a white as celly's, the black guy fucking the white guy you know so the black guy can feel like he getting get back. That makes it right to fuck a white man as long as you doing for get back. You put two whites in the cell together they not about all that fucking each other, most of them can't get into that, some of them do, most the time the one's that do pick a black celly A whole lot of this goes on in prison. I've never had a black celly. I feel like I got fucked enough from the Law men and the court system. I'm damn sure not taking dick from black or white celly, I'm not going to be the pitcher or the catcher.

Let's get back to flat land, prison. It was hard to get a shower the way the showers were set up below the staff booth on both side two Showers on each side. The Black lady C.O. sit and stand all day watch the black guys jack their dick while they watch, let a white man play with his dick, she going to watch smile and enjoy, black women like white dick too. It's a mind thing on both the black and the white race sides. Later that day after being gunned down by a hundred black guys and one white guy, the black staff writes the white guy what's called a gunning charge. That will classify him as a sex offender. I forget its ok for the black to do but not the white. That's right, the white are the racist one's in every picture even this one is you hear them tell it. It's just getting back the black can do that! Hell at flat land, when there's a line waiting on the showers that's really long most the time it is from time the cells open until lockdown that night. There's a line waiting to jack their dick, so just do it in the dayroom out in the open.

Being in this place is no more than being in a zoo. The only thing they don't they don't do like the monkeys is shit in their hand and throw it at you. They do everything else you see monkeys at the zoo. When I left the flat land, I was sent to the back woods prison. The prison I went to was white run. You would think that would be the spot for me. It turns out to be some shit too. I got a gate pass to work outside the gate. I met a guy named Gamble. All Va prisons are no smoking now and have been that way since 2012. Tobacco is worth more than gold at all Va state prisons. Suboxone is worth more than any drug or tobacco. On the streets the Suboxone clinic give people around a hundred strips a month. It's not a drug. It supposed to help people get off hard drug. That's what the flat land prison drug program is about Suboxone. From what I see people are more strung out on Suboxone than any drug I've ever seen before. It's bad in prison the prisons that have the drug programs are making a killing keeping inmates strung out on Suboxone,

At the back woods prison, they are talking about starting the drug program until they do Suboxone is not a drug but cost more than any drug I'd ever been involved with when I was out. The inmates here make a killing off Suboxone. What is free on the street each month from the Suboxone clinic a hundred strips a month, is worth $20,000 in the back wood prison. Gamble was the king pin on the tobacco product. There are not many blacks at the prison I'm talking about. They control the Suboxone supply. The whites getting more strung out every day on the black man's supply. How they get it in the prison I don't know, and I don't care. One thing about Joe Roach is I'm not in prison for telling. What I'm pissed off about is the fact that Gamble would not bring them Suboxone, so they had him busted for bringing tobacco to shut down the white man hustle. Color is more a factor now than it's ever been. Mainly on their end. If they can't get what they want they going to shut the white man down, That's what they are doing while people are so stupid and strung ant on Suboxone. They will not stick as together your own kind will throw you under the bus, just for a sixteenth of Suboxone,

Gamble had the perfect thing going on until he started doing business with the blacks. He said all he was doing was tobacco. I told him that's how it starts then they want him to bring other stuff. I told him it's not worth it. Gamble was a good guy. I hate to see him get caught up in their bullshit, I know how it works. Things went well with the tobacco product for a while, then sure enough they tried to get him to bring spice and Suboxone. When he started falling back, cause he didn't want to get involved with doing that. That's when the problems started for him and the white's selling tobacco. At first, they tried to get him to sell tobacco only to them. They had the plan to control the tobacco and the Suboxone.

They kept putting pressure on him, until he just cut them off completely. He told them he was not doing nothing not even tobacco. I told Gamble it was going to be trouble, cause the blacks knew, there was one white guy that was still getting tobacco, and Gamble was supplying It, since Gamble would not do business with them no more, they said if they couldn't control it, the whites were not going to control it. They had people from the outside to call the prison and make complaints that Gamble was putting hits on the blacks at this white ran prison. This is what the blacks do when they don't get what they want. The prison investigators knew something had to be done. Even if this was all a lie, the blacks had the upper hand by saying they felt threatened by an employee at this mostly white inmate prison, along with 98% white staff. If something wasn't done the next step for the blacks would be internal affairs, That the ace they always kept in the hole to be played next if they didn't get their way.

There are about four hundred white inmates at the prison and about a hundred blacks. None of the blacks wanted to be at the prison to begin with, using It being back wood and racist to get away with what they were doing. The prison was back woods and if they showed a white woman their black dick some would look and smile. You have some white girls like that, but some would treat them just as the whites were treated at a flat land prison and write them a charge. Of course they would use the color thing she wrote a charge. They never look at the picture like it was. They only wanted to look at it at from their point of view. It was a racist thing was the reason they could play with their dick in front of a white lady C.O. The real truth is some the white ladies like looking at a black dick. Then again you have some white women who don't want to see a black dick. My bad I forget she's racist at this white run back wood prison.

Back to Gamble. He had been working at the back wood prison for some years and never had a problem. I told him when he started doing business directly with the black's it would not be long. The way it works is just like I said it would. Color has never been a factor in my life but it's a factor now, just stop everywhere you go. Just stop and look around you. This is what the world has come to. Gamble no longer works at the back wood prison. He didn't get fired, he just quit. They were going to make it impossible for him to keep his job since he would not get on board and bring them the drugs they wanted. Whoever is reading this book, know that Gamble was never a part of any drugs. I know that as a fact, as I am a drug free Inmate. Like I told Gamble tobacco is one thing, but drugs open up a whole different door. Thats why and how I know he was not involved with bringing any Drugs to this Back wood prison. If he would have never started with the blacks he still be working here.

He had two buddies that work at the same prison with him, one was like his brother the other were both their friends. Neither of them had any knowledge of anything that was going on concerning this. The one friend that was like Gamble's brother, he never cared much for me. Even though I knew he felt that way about me, I still thought he was a ok stand up type guy. Even though he smoked my ass after Gamble left by having me put on the shittiest job at this prison, in the boiler room shoveling coal like a slave, he's still an ok guy with me.

After Gamble was gone the black's still were not satisfied. They had in their mind this friend that was like a brother to Gamble. They wanted to get rid of him and this come from the horse's mouth. The one that sunk Gamble said he felt like Gamble's friend was the one that put a hit on him. There was never a hit to begin with. When I was asked, I told nothing, I don't know anything about Gamble to begin with, as far as Gamble's best friend being involved with anything. That was nothing but a lie, just the black's trying to get him fired. The blacks were only saying this about Gambles friend because they figured they would go ahead get him out the way too. Not that he ever would bring anything, they wanted to make sure of it. Thats why they involved him. I did say I had no knowledge of Gamble bringing anything. As far as Gamble's friend that never happen and never was going to happen. Now I'm stuck at the boiler room shoveling coal permanently is what I was told. I'm sure it boils down to me not knowing nothing about nothing. Sometimes a person is still punished for keeping it real. I am fifty-two years old with four year's left. Thats a long time to be shoveling coal. I probably have black lung by time I get out. To find myself at the boiler room, I guess that's the easiest to be told I done fucked up! I'm not in prison for telling. Gamble has never brought me nothing. If being real cost me four years of hard labor so be it, I guess I'll be a coal shoveling fool for the next four years.

Color with me is still not a factor. You did what you had to do when you didn't get your way, you done nothing less than I expected you to do. That's why I'm not mad. I knew this was going to happen, regardless its nothing I could have done to stop any of you from telling the lie's that you told, This is something you got honest when you don't want the white man run prison. Seem's to me the man can't have nothing, not here or at the flat land prison, looks like the world to me either you going to run it or destroy it. You are doing a damn good job at both. No matter where you are at it looks like you plan, color is a factor. Doing the same thing that has been doing for as long as you been in this country. It's not your fault you done fucked up more than you ever fix. I wouldn't feel like this if you didn't fuck that up, you know if you read my books, I tell it like it is, I like black people usually more the white, all depends on the person or should I say situation. I do know there's a lot of black folks I like. Not until I came to prison did I ever meet a full blown nigger. What makes it so bad there are more white niggers than black. I look around me in prison, at this back wood prison, I ask myself where am I at? I know you think I'm racist but I'm not. If I am its toward my own kind more than black. The white's here do not act like convicts they act more like white niggers. They act like the world owes them more than the blacks do, I can see me getting more racist every day. I've never seen so many white dick riders as I seen here in my whole life. No wonder the white women ride black dick. What the fuck good is a white man when he's riding dick too? If doing time now don't break you from coming to prison, I can honest say nothing will. I am so done with prison life. This tour has broke me. I'm done with the drug life and everything else I use to get into. I can honestly say this is the worse time I've ever served in my life.

Now I done got older and gray. It's time to throw the towel in, Not counting the time. I done as a juvenile, just prison time, I've had to serve enough time to satisfy a two year sentence and a twenty year sentence. Thank God they were under the old Law before 1995 I only had to do a quarter of them sentences then a ten year sentence another two-year sentence and now another ten-year sentence. When I finish this one out I'll be done spent altogether twenty-two years in prison, I'll be fifty-seven years old when I get out. I'm ready to lay down and spend the last years I have left sitting around on my property in Roach town, maybe write a couple more books about a good life, I hope! Maybe spend a lot of time with my grandson, Cash, my daughter Tosha has had for me to show the love I never took time to show her or her brother Jj. They are my whole world. Jj was killed in a car wreck in 2018; In my mind and heart he will always be alive. Maybe I can spend a lot of time with Cash, that's my grandson's name and maybe I'll get to spend time with my other grandson -Jj's son Brayden at least that's my goal.

The outlaw life I think is over. If I don't stop the outlaw life now, I'll end up dying in prison, I'm not trying to do that, I've wasted most of my life behind bars.

What time I have left I need to make good of it. There's still a lot of people who don't know about me. I really know more about God than most people would think I've never asked God for any favors. I always said when I'm ready he will be there. There's been some miracles happen in my life, without him making them miracles happen I wouldn't be sitting here today. He's been keeping me alive for some reason, maybe it's because he knows me better than I know myself.

I hope my next book will bring me closer to him and everyone else that knew I wasn't really as bad as I was made out to be. My next book you will need to brace self, "The Book of Joe: The New Me."

The End

LIFE 2

JOE ROACH

www.ingramcontent.com/pod-product-compliance
Lightning Source LLC
Chambersburg PA
CBHW070912100726
47907CB00008B/2296